THE APPRENTICE

David Berardelli

THE APPRENTICE

GRAVESTONE PRESS

THE DAY BEFORE

Orlando, Florida 3:48 P.M.

His temples throbbing, Sergeant Roger Amos squeezed out of the police cruiser and screwed his service cap onto his large, square head.

The intersection was a mess.

Glass shards scattered over six lanes of highway twinkled like precious gems in the glare of the afternoon sun. Jagged pieces of metal were strewn a hundred yards from the collision. This was going to be ugly if traffic wasn't detoured. Rush hour had started nearly an hour earlier.

The stench of gas fumes and peeled rubber hung heavily in the air. Paramedics hauled the semiconscious driver from the twisted metal husk that had once been a shiny red Toyota Supra.

Farther down, traffic had already bottlenecked. With glass covering one lane the only vehicles chancing through were a mean-sounding Hog and an ancient pickup chugging away on four bald tires.

"Drunk's gonna be just fine." Rivera trotted over, his knife-blade-thin frame easily dodging the slow-passing ambulance. "Couple scratches and a bloody nose, maybe a cracked rib or two. His alcohol level's gotta be sky high. We'll take good care of him till it's time to get him to trial."

Amos was having trouble holding down the rage. At his last physical his doctor clucked over him like a mother hen. That same old lecture about

5

high blood pressure being the silent killer and that he wouldn't see retirement in the next five years if he didn't learn to mellow.

But this was too much. Some poor Joe coming home from work and getting in the way of someone who shouldn't be anywhere near a steering wheel. Amos had lost several friends and a brother-in-law under similar circumstances.

"What tears me up," he told Rivera, "is the poor slob who got in the way when that drunk tore through the red light. Guy was just trying to make it home in one piece after a hard day at the office. Too damn much to hope for these days."

Rivera shook his head. "I just hope they'll be able to cut him out of the Mustang."

The squealing ambulance from Orlando Regional rocked to a halt, flashers lighting the littered roadway. Its paramedics jumped out to join the first group. Removing the driver from the smashed green Mustang was going to be a chore.

"I gotta see this." His nightstick tapping his thigh, Amos jogged over to the wreckage.

The car was mashed into a grotesque horseshoe. The trunk lid, slammed open at impact, dangled at an odd angle, scraping the macadam. Two paramedics huddled near the driver's side. Two broad-shouldered men working the Jaws of Life forced the passenger's door open. A slender Latina woman, her black hair tied in a thick ponytail, hopped down from the rear of the ambulance and pushed a gurney over to the group.

Amos reached them as they laid the driver carefully onto the gurney.

Glass and metal debris covered the man's shirt, tie, and trousers. Metal flecks glistened in his blood-matted dark-brown hair. His head and neck were immobilized in a yellow neck brace strapped to the gurney. Once his left arm and leg were stabilized, a young male paramedic tended to the bleeding while his older partner flushed the glass carefully from the victim's closed eyes and fitted an oxygen mask over his face.

"Any chance?" Amos asked.

The older paramedic gently swabbed away the last of the tiny fragments. "Never know. He could pull out of it. He seems to be in pretty good shape."

"What's the scenario?"

The paramedics pushed the gurney toward the ambulance. "Massive internal damage," the older one said. "Some arteries were severed but we got them clamped for the time being. I'm worried about his head injuries. Hit it pretty hard when the Toyota slammed into him. Can't tell for sure but looks like his neck snapped. There's a pulse…" He shook his head.

From the other side of the road the drunk driver yelled something incoherent while the paramedics raised his gurney before shoving it into the ambulance. Amos wanted to shut him up permanently with his billy club. One of these days the courts would stop messing around with these idiots and put them away for good.

The victim opened one eye.

Amos bent over, leaning close. It was best to sound hopeful. A little optimism might help. "Hey, fella. You with us?"

The victim managed a faint smile under the mask.

Amos tapped the younger paramedic's arm. "He's smilin'..."

The rear doors were pulled open wider.

Amos stayed close. "Say something, fella."

The man's lips parted. Beneath the collective roar of idling traffic, sirens, cops, angry drivers, and harried paramedics, the only word Amos could distinguish was something that sounded like "Philadelphia."

"What was that?" Amos reached for the mask. "He's tryin' to talk."

"Leave that alone." The paramedic grabbed his wrist. "It's helping him breathe."

"But I can't hear what—"

"Doesn't matter."

Amos ignored the comment. "Hey, fella. They're gonna take real good care of you. They'll be taking you to ORMC. They'll know exactly what to do. Got doctors all over the place, specialists— the works. You'll be there in just a few minutes. You'll get everything you need. Understand?"

No response.

"C'mon." The paramedic rapped him on the beefy shoulder. "We gotta go."

Amos clasped the man's wrist, searching for a pulse.

It was very weak. "Can you hear me, fella?"

The man's eyes closed.

Amos could feel the heat gathering in his neck. The poor guy was slipping away.

Goddamn drunks. "You'll…be okay." His heart pounded. He kept talking even as the ambulance doors slammed in his face. "They'll take real good care of you. You'll be…just fine. They'll know what to do. You hear me?"

***

"Rand?"

A shimmering white shape. "Can you hear me?"

Smoke whirled around the approaching form. Pieces of shadows sputtered before his eyes.

A difficult day at the office—computer glitches, angry customers, unnecessary meetings, conference calls. Sitting in the conference room, his reps duking it out while he zoned out and watched the clear-blue Orlando skyline. Isolated in his own little sphere, wondering why he didn't sell the company and find a quiet place where he could sit out his days on his back porch, listening to his CD collection. He'd been in the work force most of his life and had been burned out for as long as he could remember. The company had been doing well the last five years but he knew there had to be more to life than a healthy stock portfolio, a substantial checking account and a Money Market fund.

Shouldn't he be enjoying life?

The faces of the reps meshed into one, clouding over and turning into the road ahead as he drove back to his apartment.

The heavy Orlando traffic—a sprawling mass of restlessness—roared and growled around him. The drivers were anonymous and anxious in their fast-moving, heavily tinted sanctuaries.

Vehicles pulled up alongside him, eased back, cut in behind and in front, zigzagged, and roared away. License plates from every state blended into a collage of irritation.

A deafening, growing roar erupted on his left. A loud, sickening crunch forced his head against the driver's window. A large red blur pushed against him, screaming before plunging into the Mustang. A colossal burst of intense heat exploded down his limbs. A scorching rupture of blinding pain turned everything dark and gooey.

The blackness gradually lifted, leaving only the heat and the pain.

Blurry shadows. Banging noises. Whisperings.

A cornucopia of smells.

A bulky blue shape bent over him. A shiny black plastic nametag—*Amos*—glinted before his eyes. Large, big-knuckled hands opened and closed nervously. A strong mix of sweat, exhaust fumes, and stale coffee floated lazily past.

Clouds appeared, dimming the shadows. The pain ebbed. A glittering rainbow dazzled the sky, smearing it with neon.

The bulky figure lightened, then dimmed, the smells around it growing faint. More whisperings. The scents changed, grew sweeter, the clouds thicker, warmer. Where Amos was standing, a slender vision in a flowing white robe appeared in the whirling clouds.

The smoke cleared.

A beautiful woman with long white hair the same texture as down, smooth alabaster skin, and bright blue eyes came into view. As the vision neared, warmth filled his being. The intense pain disappeared. He wanted to know where the pain had gone—what sort of healing powers this strange creature possessed.

"Can you hear me, Rand?"

He found his voice. "You ...know my name?"

"I know all about you." The creature's bright blue eyes glistened. They stayed on him, showing both fear and concern. For a moment he wondered if he'd seen her before.

A restless white mist surrounded them. There was nothing to be seen beyond it.

"Come with me," the beautiful creature said softly. "Where?"

"You'll see."

The prospect of entering the eerie whiteness frightened him. Fear of the unknown. He'd dreaded the dark as a child and would not enter the basement of his parents' home at night. All sorts of creatures lurked down there. Creepy little things hiding behind the hot water heater or behind the cabinets. Monsters. Rats. Vampire bats. Hordes of scary things craving the tender flesh of a small boy.

But this was different. Darkness was nowhere to be seen. Light abounded. Yet he feared it.

"You must come with me." Her mouth formed a grim line; a crescent-shaped dimple appeared on either side of her full lips.

Where was he? What place was this?

"Why?" he asked.

"It'll be explained."

"When?"

Her long white hair swished quietly across her robe. "They told me you'd be difficult."

"Who?"

"Let's just say I know all about you."

"You know I'm difficult?"

"Among other things."

"My mother must be spreading rumors again."

"They're obviously not rumors…"

"Dad must be around somewhere, too."

"Perhaps…"

Something just occurred to him. "Mom and Dad are dead…"

"Really?"

He could tell by her tone that she was playing with him. "If …*you* know them, then you must—"

"C'mon. Your questions will be answered later."

"Who *are* you?"

"My name is Harriet."

"You look like the Ghost of Christmas Past. Not the one with Alistair Sim—the version with Reginald Owen. The one with Sim had a nasty-looking old man in a really tacky dress. But in the older version, that ghost was a sexy babe—"

"That's right. You're a movie buff. Lucky me…"

"She was a fox. Her hair was probably dyed. Yours isn't, is it?"

"Hardly. Listen to me…"

"You're not gonna say 'take my hand,' are you? That's what they usually said in those old fantasy flicks."

"Will you please *listen* to me?"

"She was also in that Danny Kaye movie. The one about Walter Mitty? She was a real bitch in that one. Had this ratty little dog that wanted to eat Danny Kaye. But her hair was darker, and she wasn't nearly as sexy or—"

"*Enough* strolling down Trivia Avenue. Take my hand."

"Couldn't see *that* one coming."

"I'm serious."

"Now is it time for me to say I'm a mortal? And that I'm liable to fall?"

"Not really…"

"Too tacky?"

"No…"

"Why, then?"

"It doesn't pertain to us."

"Lovely. So where are you taking me?"

"Later."

"I don't know if I should trust you."

"Why shouldn't you?"

"Women have been getting me in trouble since I was a kid."

Her milky features tightened. The blue sapphires flared. Despite her tension, the trace of a dimple remained at each corner of her mouth. He wondered if they ever disappeared completely.

"I really don't think you have much choice here."

"Where's a cop when you need one?" Then he remembered. "That's right. The last one I saw was trying to pull off my mask. That idiot. Doesn't the Police Department hire people with brain cells anymore?"

"Shut up and take my hand."

"You sure are pushy." He did as she said. A flurry of heat traveled up his arm.

Everything grew fuzzy.

THE FIRST DAY

CHAPTER 1

Leaning against the chipped counter in her light-blue smock, the faces streaming past the front window of the Five'n Dime, Nadine Connelly couldn't help wondering if anyone was as depressed as she was.

She saw worry in some, impatience in others, still others deep in thought. She realized how deceptive and unreliable facial expressions could be. Some people just didn't want their battles to show. But no matter what she saw, she suspected everyone had something going on that was far from pleasant.

Ralph, his grin big and bright, burst into the store. He was wearing his best suit and smelling like he'd taken a bath in *Stetson*—which told her he had some important wheeling and dealing lined up for the afternoon.

"Hey, babe." He gave her his usual peck on the cheek. A thick wave of *Stetson*, Colgate, and *Aramis Hair Malt* brushed her face. The mixture was even stronger than usual. It told her that whatever he'd lined up probably involved a woman. Ralph preferred dealing with women; he said he always felt more relaxed around them. "Got any spare change?"

It had been three days since she'd received the results of her tests. Ralph had been back home for five days but had been too busy to spend much time with her. He was gone most of the day and came home long after she'd gone to bed. It made her think he'd only come back because he needed a place to crash.

"Ralph, we need to talk."

"Can't now, babe. Got an appointment near the Country Club." His grin flashed even brighter. "You know what that means?"

"It means you're too busy to talk," she said flatly.

"This is important. If I can flip that townhouse, we'll make a fortune."

"Did you forget that we're about to lose our *own* home?"

He shook his head the way he usually did when he didn't want her changing the subject. "When I make this one, we'll have two hundred K in our bank account. I figure six weeks, tops. I even have the crew picked out. An outfit that works out of St. Clairsville. A real class bunch of guys. We can toss some pocket change at old Abner. That ought to cool his heels with the foreclosure."

She wanted Ralph to know that he was an idiot if he thought he could make that kind of money that fast. But it wouldn't accomplish anything. She'd tried reasoning with him before. When he was all worked up about something, he was like a little kid with his first bicycle.

"You haven't even asked about my tests."

He patted her arm. "You're as healthy as a horse, babe. You're also beautiful, with a smile that could bring a dead man back to life." He reached behind her, where she kept her purse on the shelf beneath the register. "I could use a couple of twenties if you've got 'em. Just in case I've got to wine and dine Ms. Hayworth."

"Who?"

"The realtor I told you about?" His brows mashed together. "Don't tell me you've forgotten *already*?"

"Other stuff on my mind, I guess." She pulled her purse from his grasp and opened it. She found two twenties, two tens, a five and some ones. The money was supposed to be for groceries, but she knew how that would go over. You didn't argue with Ralph, you just let him go. Besides, the store was filling up and she didn't want anyone to know their business.

He beat her to the draw, his hand moving like lightning, the twenties trapped between thumb and index finger, then stuck into a trouser pocket even before she could focus. "Thanks, babe. You won't be sorry. I'll wrap this up in an hour and you'll be bragging about me all over town." He planted another quick kiss on her cheek, spun around and was gone in seconds.

His departure no longer caused the same heavy throbbing of emptiness she'd experienced years earlier.

It was no wonder. In their five years together, Ralph had left four times. The reasons were always the same: Barnes cramped his style. The big cities were where his future patiently awaited his grand arrival. There was nothing in Barnes but small-town businesses and small-minded people.

However, his reasons for coming back were always different. He hadn't been able to raise enough investment capital. It was the wrong time of year. The Stock Market had made things tight. Politicians. The Economy. The price of gas.

Nadine took him back every time. She never once thought otherwise. Her parents were always together when she was growing up, even through the bad times, when Daddy lost his job and the money stopped coming in. Families stuck together, as Momma always said. That's the way things were. You married your man for better or for worse. That's what was wrong with the world now. Not enough ladies sticking by their men. Everyone was too concerned with having fun and unaware that life wasn't just fun, it was a lot of other things, too.

All men have things wrong with them, Momma told her. If they're pretty, they want to spread it around for everyone to appreciate. If they're not, they're resentful about it and take it out on everyone. They sometimes need a helping hand, sometimes a nurse, and sometimes a shoulder to cry on. There are times when they need common sense pounded into them. You can't do that if you don't take them back.

She did what Momma suggested. She took Ralph back. Momma would be pleased if she was still alive. Daddy would be, too. In fact, everyone would be pleased.

Everyone but Nadine, who knew that even though she kept taking Ralph back, the love she once had for him would never come back.

The clock on the wall said it was an hour before lunchtime. Good. Pretty soon she could enjoy her first break. She lived for breaks these days. The downside was that they gave her too much time to think. And she didn't want to think too much because it depressed her.

When she was depressed, it was hard to be pleasant, to smile at the customers.

She needed to present a positive image. To give everyone the illusion everything was right with the world. Which was stupid because everything was *not* right. You knew it and they knew it.

"Hi, Nadie." Gertie Williamson pulled her items out of the small blue cart and piled them on the counter. "And how're we doing this sunny day?"

"Just fine, thanks." Nadine switched her smile back on—more as a convenience than anything else. She didn't want anyone to know that at this very moment, the young woman behind it was not doing very well at all and didn't care if the sun was up there or not.

"I saw your hubby." Mrs. Williamson winked. "Nice-looking, and boy, does that man know how to dress..."

"It's one of his favorite things." She hoped she hadn't sounded too bitter.

"Wish *my* hubby could look nice occasionally. I'm lucky he pulls on a shirt on weekends when he's glued to the armchair in front of the boob tube, watching that stupid Sports Channel."

Nadine gathered up Mrs. Williamson's purchases. Two black wire brassieres—both obviously much too small for the husky lady. Two pairs of oversized black slacks. A small box of chocolate-covered cherries and two Diet Cokes.

"I'm confused about the bras." A tight frown settled in between Mrs. Williamson's chubby cheeks. "They were in the Bargain Bin, but I'm not sure if the tags are right. One didn't have its yellow sticker, but since they're both the same, I figured they'd be the same price."

Nadine glanced at the sales flyer taped to the side of the register. Usually, she didn't have to double-check. She'd always been able to keep such unimportant things in her head. Which was even more proof that her life reeked. "They're still on sale. One of the clerks forgot to switch the tags or it came off when someone was going through the pile."

"So they're ten percent off, then?"

"Absolutely." She keyed them in manually and put them in a bag. "In fact, Artie said something about adding another five to it tomorrow, but he got sidetracked. I'll ring up the extra. He won't mind."

"You sure? Don't wanna get you in trouble."

"Artie's always too swamped to take care of everything. Besides, he doesn't like it when we can't move the stock fast enough."

"That's sweet of you, Nadie. Thank you."

"No prob." She rang everything up and pulled more plastic bags from a drawer.

Mrs. Williamson's frown drifted back. "Been getting enough sleep?"

"Pardon?"

"Don't mind me saying so, you've been looking tired the last few days."

"I'm fine, thanks."

"Heard you went to the hospital last week. Anything wrong?"

Actually, everything in the world was wrong, but she was determined not to tell anyone. It wouldn't help, and it sure wouldn't make her feel any better. And if Ralph wasn't concerned, why should anyone else care?

"Just a checkup." She made sure her smile stayed right where it was.

"Well, some of us have noticed you haven't been your normal happy self. Hope you're not coming down with something."

It was obviously going to take more of an effort to keep her smile turned on. Otherwise, she'd have to do a lot more lying. "No, really. I'm fine."

"I dunno." Mrs. Williamson sounded skeptical. "You can't be too sure—especially when you deal with the public all day long. I was at the bank two weeks ago, just for a small withdrawal—you know, spending money, groceries, that sort of thing—and I start gettin' sick soon as I get home—coughing, hacking away, sweats. I was only in that bank five minutes and there were three, maybe four folks there, but there I was, sick before I knew it."

"You're okay now, I hope." The last thing she needed was a cold.

Mrs. Williamson grinned broadly. "No need to worry. I wouldn't expose you if I was still contagious. I was taught better than that." She waved, then snatched up her bags and waddled out of the store.

The clock said 11:11. The morning was dragging like a dying cockroach. All she could think of was driving home and getting out of these clothes. Hopefully Ralph would be home for dinner, and they could talk. He needed to know about her test results. They also had to talk about doing something that would help them keep the house. Even if Ralph's scheme turned out, it was going to be weeks before they saw any profit from it. The bank wanted their money in five days.

Her eyes welled up even before she realized it. She reached around for the yellow plastic chain to block off the aisle so she could rush to the restroom and have a quick cry.

CHAPTER 2

The clouds thinned.

A crisp brown autumn day peppered the countryside. A snort of cool wind rushing up the valley scattered dead leaves across the macadam. The air had that rich sweet smell that tells you winter isn't far away.

Rand Powell had driven this crumbling two-lane road fifteen years ago. The aging frame houses facing the street forced open the dusty door of memory. Fresh paint applied to doorways, garages, and shutters could not disguise the picture.

But as overwhelming as this was, it wasn't the only thing on his mind.

"I'm actually dead?" he asked the beautiful white-haired creature walking beside him. "Really and truly *dead*?"

"I'm afraid so."

"No longer living? Stone cold?"

"You got it."

The contentment in her eyes disturbed him. "You don't have to sound so *happy* about it…"

"Just telling how it is."

"So *that's* why that Orlando cop was so bummed out…"

"By the way, what did you tell him?"

"I was trying to say I'd rather be living in Philadelphia. But since my neck was broken and most of my ribs were cracked, my lung power wasn't what it should have been."

23

"I…don't understand."

"When your ribs are cracked and your neck is broken, you don't exactly feel like jumping up and—"

"Oh, I get *that* part."

"What *don't* you get?"

"The Philadelphia thing."

"It's sort of a W.C. Fields quote. Apparently he said, 'I would rather be living in Philadelphia.'"

"Ah. *More* movie trivia."

"I'm a walking showcase."

Harriet brushed some silken hair away from her face. "What did that traffic accident have to do—"

"I was pissed and didn't want to be loaded into an ambulance right then. Just a little humor to ease the moment."

"Humor? At a traffic accident?"

"I was always fun at parties, too."

"But at a *traffic accident*?"

"The cop was stressed out. And he was large…"

"So?"

"I was worried he'd have a coronary and there wouldn't be enough room in the ambulance for both of us."

"How thoughtful."

"It's part of my psyche. My dad did a few good deeds while Mom was pregnant with me."

"I knew there had to be *some* explanation…"

He led the way around a bend. The road went straight.

The sign

was stuck into the ground off the shoulder.

"Dead, eh?" It certainly was difficult to swallow.

"Yes, Rand. I'm sorry."

"And I thought my day couldn't get worse…"

But there were too many other explanations. Logical ones. Things much easier to accept.

He'd had a couple of martinis for lunch that day. Or was it three? Right now, he couldn't remember. It was no wonder. How could you coax your brain into working at all when you were just told you were dead?

What happened during the drive home might not have been as bad as he thought. He could be lying in a hospital bed, the medication making him dream all this. He might have steered clear of the Toyota, made it back to the apartment and had a couple of strong drinks to celebrate his brush with death. He was jittery—that could have been one messy accident—and needed more than two to calm down. That was the thing about drinking to calm down. Sometimes you were knocked flat on your ass.

But even if he *was* dead, and Harriet *wasn't* lying, some things just didn't add up.

"How come I don't *feel* dead?"

"What did you expect?"

"It's hard to imagine anything when you see someone lying in a casket. I'm no rocket scientist, but there just doesn't seem to be too much going on in one of those things."

"My, we're observant this morning."

"I've heard so much hype about it over the years— Catechism class, high school, college. But no one ever convinced me of anything."

"No one's supposed to know until his time comes," Harriet said.

"Good policy."

"I'm glad you approve."

"You just can't trust people. Tell your best friend about a beautiful, secluded place you found in the mountains. Next time you go there, you'll see cars all over the damned place, travel trailers, ATVs, satellite dishes, screaming kids, a strip mall…and, of course, Wal-Mart."

"Cynical, aren't we?"

He looked down at himself and shook his head. It was time to have more questions answered. "Tell me about this body." He held out his hands. "These ain't mine."

"How can you tell?"

"The thumbs are different."

She blinked. "You know your thumbs?"

"Mine were double-jointed. I could always wiggle them. It made my aunts queasy, and my uncles laugh." He tried doing it, but they wouldn't cooperate. "See there? Nothing."

"You *are* observant."

"Everyone knows his own hands."

"Well, now you know. It's borrowed."

"What? The thumbs?"

"The whole package."

"*Borrowed*?"

"Yes."

"Why?"

"Yours was, well, slightly damaged."

"Getting creamed in traffic does tend to leave a mark."

"We needed a temporary vessel. Like yours so you'd feel comfortable."

"Where'd you pick it up? They have *stores* for this?"

"Don't be silly. The man is homeless."

"And he doesn't know what's going on?"

"Of course not. He's presently sleeping."

"On his own?"

"Hypnotically."

"And he's going to come out of it?"

"Of course. We're not savages, you know."

"I certainly hope he doesn't wake up while I'm walking around inside him."

"He won't."

"You're sure?"

"Absolutely."

"What about this wardrobe—and I use the term loosely." The well-worn jacket, frayed corduroys, and smudged tennis shoes didn't make him feel comfortable at all.

"What's wrong with it?"

"It's sort of neo-tacky, and reeks of Skid Row."

"Can you please be more specific?"

"I thought I was."

"What don't you like about it?"

"I'd like to be subtle, but I don't really think I can and still get my point across. When you guys found this ensemble, were you maybe in the wrong end of town? Or didn't you have time to shop around for something more fashionable? Something with flare? Casual, yet classy enough for the busy exec-about-town who just died but still wants to keep up his snappy appearance? Something, maybe, without *patches*?"

"We don't want you attracting attention."

"And you think Freddie the Freeloader will blend into the background?"

"People don't usually notice poorly dressed folks. Do I have to remind you that this man is homeless?"

"I'm liable to be arrested for vagrancy."

"I'll try and keep you safe."

"Look at this. Tennis shoes with a corduroy jacket? Jeans?"

Harriet sighed. "We didn't really have a lot of time…"

"All I need is a stupid white hat. Then I'll look like Kolchak."

"Who?"

"The guy in Night Stalker."

"Night Stalker?"

"Never mind."

Harriet nodded. "*More* movie stuff…"

"TV."

"Same thing."

"This is a big-time culture shock for me. First the dead thing, then a walking ad for Feed the

Homeless. I ran a *software company*, for God's sake. I had a wardrobe. Custom-fitted, the right colors—everything tasteful and in style. Hundred-dollar ties. Italian shoes. Twelve-hundred-dollar suits. This makes me want to find a tin cup, grab the nearest street corner, and blow into a kazoo."

"Like I said, it's only temporary."

"How temporary?"

"Think you can put up with it for three days?"

"What happens in three days?"

"We finish our mission and move on."

"Then what?"

"We'll talk about it later."

A lime-green, primer-covered TransAm roared by, two teen boys yelling through the open window as the vehicle squealed around the corner.

"When I was their age, I was gigging in nightclubs," he said.

"That's right, you were a musician."

"A good one, too."

"What happened?"

He shrugged. "What else? Life and its many surprises."

More cars roared by.

"Can anyone but me see you?" he asked.

"No."

"Why not?"

"I'm an angel."

"Sure you're not that ghost?"

She shook her head. Her long silken hair slid across her shoulders. "It was a *movie*, Rand…"

"You sure look like her."

29

"I hope that's meant to be a compliment…"

"You didn't see the movie?"

"So long ago, I can't remember."

"Didn't I say she was a fox?"

"I think so."

"Then it was a compliment."

A sigh. "Thank you…"

"Why so skeptical?"

"I'm never quite sure just what you mean…"

"Don't trust me, eh?"

"Not really."

"You sound like you know me pretty well."

A pause. "That could very well be…"

Once again he wondered who she'd talked to. The way her big blue eyes had settled on his made him suspicious. "Must've been quite a bull session up there."

"We don't call them that."

"Whatever you call them, I'll bet it was interesting."

"*I'll* never tell."

"I'm *so* lucky. I'm with a female who clams up when you want her to talk."

"If I told you everything, none of this would be fun."

"Then you must be saving the real chuckles for later."

She tilted her head. "I thought we were having fun getting to know one another."

"I guess you could say that…"

"You're not enjoying my company?"

"Of course I am. Absolutely. Lots of rib-splitting entertainment. Fun. Laughs galore. Whoever said dying was the pits didn't know what he was talking—"

"You don't have to be obnoxious."

Giant buckeyes towering around the next bend blocked out the sun. An elderly man in a flannel jacket and loose corduroy pants raked leaves in the front yard of a large two-story brick farmhouse. He pulled the straw hat from his bald scalp and dabbed at his glistening forehead with a checkered handkerchief.

A giant question popped up. "How come I'm here?"

"Where else would you be?"

"You know. That *other* place. A lot darker, hotter, and smellier. Being coaxed along by a big ugly brute with a long, unpronounceable Latin name and bad breath from drooling."

Her blue sapphires blinked. "Where *do* you get these strange ideas?"

He shrugged. "Comic books. A healthy imagination. The Catholic Church."

"What makes you think you're destined to go there?"

"I don't know. I wasn't exactly the world's greatest guy, you know."

"Really?"

"I ran a company. I had to fire people, be mean to them. I even had affairs."

"With women?"

"Of course."

31

"Not with men at all?"

"Of course not."

"Why not?"

"I like women. Period."

Harriet nodded. "I know."

"You do?"

"Of course."

"That's right, you know a lot about me. But none of this answers my question."

"Which one?"

"The one about why I'm here."

"You're needed here."

"I'm supposed to spend eternity in Barnes, Ohio?"

"Not eternity—"

"That's right. Three days."

"Your mother was right. You really *are* intelligent."

"She tells everyone I take after her side of the family."

Straight ahead, the Burger King stood boldly on the crest of the hill.

Rand grew silent.

"Something wrong?"

Rand kept his eyes focused on the path in front of him.

He didn't reply.

About a minute later Harriet said, "What about that house we just passed?"

"Which one?"

"The big one on the corner."

He was silent for a moment. "What makes you think—"

"You stepped down from the curb and were nearly sideswiped by that passing car. You also closed your eyes and tensed up. Your closed fists also gave me a tiny clue."

He could tell by her dark expression that she was already figuring out the situation. Intelligent women had always scared him, made him feel vulnerable. Why should things be any different after death? "I lived on the first floor."

"How long?"

"Two years."

"Anything else bothering you?"

"The Burger King."

"What about it?"

"It's strange, coming back after all these years. Everything feels the same."

Before they turned the corner, he glanced behind them.

"Something else?" Harriet asked.

He thought just for a moment that he'd seen the flash of a blond pigtail but knew it was just his imagination. "Just checking to make sure the past hasn't caught up to me," he said softly.

Two- and three-story houses lining the street stretched down the hill, where the downtown area spread out for four square blocks. Mailboxes, hedges, and parked cars covered both sides of the avenue. Elderly people lounged on front porches, enjoying the cool morning.

Across the street, a large three-story brick with the sign, *Dennison's Music Society* nailed to the front door, anchored the block. A smaller painted sign, *"private lessons for young and old, all instruments—inquire inside,"* swayed over the front porch.

Next to it, a shop advertised *Otis's Novelties* in red lettering over the shuttered entrance. A man with thinning white hair hunkered in the storefront window, positioning the resin sculpture of a large gray Arabian horse for display.

"Where we going?" he asked.

"Keep walking."

"You don't like answering questions, do you?"

"If I told you specifics—"

"I know. It would ruin the fun for later."

Harriet nearly smiled. "By golly, he's finally getting it!"

34

CHAPTER 3

Frowning at the interruption, Montgomery Niemus picked up the phone.

How the hell was he supposed to concentrate on his new project if he had to stop every fifteen minutes to answer the phone? Lorraine knew he didn't want to be disturbed. If this wasn't an emergency, he was going to call her in here and remind her that he wasn't paying her twenty bucks an hour just because she had a great set of legs. That certainly didn't hurt the situation, but it wouldn't help him at all if she didn't obey his instructions.

"Yes?"

"I'm sorry, Mr. Niemus, but you've got a visitor."

"Lorraine, I specifically told you I didn't want to be interrupted."

"I know that, sir. And I'm really sorry, but Mr. Connelly says it's urgent."

"Ralph Connelly?"

"Yes, Mr. Niemus."

Being interrupted was one thing; but when the interruption turned out to be a loser like Connelly... "Tell him I'm horribly busy."

"I did."

"So why are we having this conversation?"

"He...insists on talking to you."

Monty glanced at his Rolex. Some people had more balls than brains. Connelly was just another small-minded weasel with big ideas. He also happened to be married to the best-looking woman in town—which made Monty dislike him even more. And the fact that he still owed Monty a grand from over a year ago sealed the idiot's doom.

So why did the idiot want to talk?

To beg for more money for another outlandish scheme?

Or was it something else?

Anything was possible. Despite his misgivings, this was something he might as well find out about. If Connelly had the money, it would be foolish to send him away. Besides, Connelly had the nasty habit of hounding you to death when you tried snubbing him.

"Send him in." He hoped he wasn't making a big mistake.

Connelly came in dressed in his customary off-the-rack Brooks Brothers special. The room instantly grew thick with the sweet scent of his knock-off brand of cologne. His glistening white teeth, as usual, made Monty want to grab his Foster Grants to shield his eyes from the glare.

Monty had never cared for lowlifes who tried projecting an image of wealth and breeding—two qualities that couldn't be fabricated. Monty himself had a humble background but had left the farm as soon as he possibly could. He'd financed his own business school education, taught himself how to invest, developed a sixth sense with his dealings and made his first million by the time he was twenty-five. During the last fifteen years he had increased his wealth a hundredfold. He'd diversified, shifting into real estate, and generating a fortune through raw land and all sorts of acquisitions. He'd built up a huge stock portfolio and accumulated a lot of cash. Buildings. Antique cars. Gold coins. He'd done it by himself. And he hadn't succeeded by ignoring his debts. Connelly was just another starry-eyed hopeful wanting to join the ranks of the rich. He knew how to dress well on a budget and project the illusion of knowledge, but anyone familiar with the man knew it was an act.

Connelly had no idea how to amass wealth the proper way.

"Good of you to see me on such short notice, Mr. Niemus."

Monty took the offered hand and made it brief. He gestured for Connelly to sit. "So, what brings you here? I take it you've finally come to pay me back that thousand."

"Better than that."

Sighing, Monty unbuttoned his Armani jacket and sat back. Some people really had the nerve. Knowing Connelly as he did, this sounded like another get-rich-quick scheme—which, in Connelly's case, also meant backing. This idiot had actually come to ask for more money.

"I guess I don't have to tell you how lenient I've been, holding prosecution for an extended debt—"

"And I appreciate it—I truly do. But I've come to offer you a proposition, one that will be of great benefit to both of us."

Monty rested his elbows on the table. He didn't trust Connelly. However, if there was a possible business venture in the works, he was eager to learn about it. "I'm listening. But bear in mind, I'm skeptical. We've been through this before."

"It's about my house on Main and Elm. The one standing in your way of the Elm Street Condominium Project."

This was interesting. The fact that Connelly suddenly appeared dead-serious told Monty this might indeed be worth looking into. But there was still one huge factor that was certain to gum up the works.

"You mean the house that's in your wife's name?"

"That's the one."

"What about it?"

Connelly's gleaming grin returned. "What would you say if I told you I'm about to hand it to you on a silver platter?"

CHAPTER 4

Rand reluctantly followed Harriet up the cracked stone walk.

The Catholic Church of Saint William had changed very little. The same soot-covered block, the same gloomy entrance. The double wooden doors, heavy with dark stain, were as smudged and chipped as they were fifteen years earlier. It was here that Father Martin, tall and broad-shouldered, his bright smile in direct contrast with his dark robes, appeared after each sermon, shaking hands, and greeting his loyal parishioners.

One sunny morning, after exchanging pleasantries with an elderly man in a wheelchair, Father Martin turned to Rand, who was walking back to his car.

"Haven't seen you before, young man. Do you live in town? Or just passing through?"

"I live here."

"How long?"

"Two months."

"And this is your first time in our church?"

"I'm afraid so."

"I sincerely hope I see you here again. It's not that much of a sacrifice, giving God an hour of your time once a week, is it?"

"Aren't you coming in?" Harriet asked.

He was watching the street. Facing the building and its memories wasn't making this any easier. "I'd rather not."

"What's the problem?"

"Don't want to see the priest."

"He won't recognize you in your new covering." A faint frown showed on her face. "Why so uncomfortable?"

"I stopped getting along with priests when I got older and started using my brain."

"We're not going inside to debate with the priest."

"I'm still down on churches."

"Thank you for clarifying things."

"The whole concept bothers me."

"Going to church doesn't automatically make you a good man. Everyone knows that."

"But I was a Catholic. You know how they are about guilt."

"I've heard that it's very important to them."

"Hell, they invented it."

"Well, since you never really went out of your way to hurt anyone—other than a few love-struck women— you're a good man."

Her statement twanged a nerve. "Love-struck women?"

"You never married."

"No…"

"No one ever touched your heart?"

"Of course someone touched my heart."

"But you didn't marry her."

"No."

"Then you must have hurt her."

"Hurt works both ways, you know…"

Harriet crossed her arms and looked obstinate.

"With women, things aren't always that simple," he said.

"They could be. If you'd put away that stupid male pride, of course."

He was suddenly suspicious. "Who have you been talking to up there?"

"Enough chitchat. C'mon. This should only take a minute."

***

Tiered white candles flickered on the tarnished brass stand, casting shadows on the stucco wall behind the Communion bench.

A sculpted crucifix, highlighted by a row of small floods, hung from the vaulted ceiling by large chains. Life-sized statues of Jesus Christ, St. Joseph, Mary, St. Jude, and Michael the Archangel posed on marble pedestals, their expressions changing in the waves of the late morning sun filtering through the stained-glass windows.

Harriet approached the Communion bench. Kneeling before the brass stand, she placed her index finger above a burning flame. She held it still until a slim two-inch glow of wavy gold grew above it, then carefully applied it to several candles.

"*Damn…*" Rand's jaw dropped.

"Promised some friends I'd light candles for them," she whispered. She shook out the flame and rose.

"How do you do that?"

"Outside. Shouldn't be talking in here anyway."

A few yards from the vestibule, a short, square man around sixty appeared, his hands clasped together in front of his ample belly, a cherubic smile on his smooth round face. "May I help you?"

"Just lighting candles."

"If you'd come for confession, you'd have to wait till Saturday at around seven P.M."

"I'm afraid confessions won't help at this stage of my career," Rand said.

The man's smile dropped abruptly. "It's never too late, young man."

"It is when you're already—"

Harriet elbowed him in the side.

"Everything all right?" the priest asked.

"Just this slight irritation I've had ever since I left Orlando."

"Orlando, Florida?"

"It's the only Orlando I'm aware of. . . ."

His tiny blue eyes beamed. "I've got a younger sister living there."

"A small world, isn't it?" He hoped the priest wouldn't do the inevitable and ask if he knew her.

"Perhaps you know her," the priest said. "She works at Orlando Regional Medical Center. She's an anesthesiologist."

Rand wanted to tell him he didn't remember anyone because he'd died before the ambulance had brought him there.

He suddenly realized that something was different. "Where's Father Martin?"

"You haven't been here for some time, I take it?"

"Not in fifteen years."

"Father Martin's passed on. He died several years ago. Close to ten, if I remember correctly."

Damn. Leave it to a priest to die and make you feel guilty even though there was nothing to feel guilty about.

The priest was studying his clothes, no doubt wondering if they'd been taken from the Goodwill box out back.

"You're Catholic?" he asked hopefully.

"I was born Catholic."

"No longer practicing?"

"Not for a long time."

"But you've come to light candles."

Rand sighed. He'd often wondered if priests were actually frustrated psychiatrists.

He wanted to tell the irritating little guy he wasn't the one lighting the damned candles. The feisty invisible chick standing beside him was the one with the magic finger.

"Actually, I'm a practicing pyromaniac."

"Pardon me?"

"Gotta stay in practice. You never know when you'll be invited to a weenie roast, and no one's brought along any fire-making implements."

"Practicing pyromaniac?" Harriet asked outside.

"He was bugging me."

"And that was all you could think of to say?"

"It was either that or introduce the two of you and let nature take its course."

"Cute."

"So tell me. That deal with your finger. What was that all about?"

"Like I said, I light candles for friends whenever I get the chance. And by the way, watch your language—especially in a *church*."

"Sorry. I saw your finger spitting flame and my iron nerve just fizzled away. How'd you do it?"

"It's not hard. You'll be doing it yourself before long. Angels have interesting but limited powers."

"One other thing."

"What's that?"

"*Why'd* you do it?"

"Didn't see any matches lying around. Did you?"

CHAPTER 5

As he cruised up the winding drive, Ralph Connelly strongly suspected that Rachel Hayworth was going to be easy to deal with.

You could tell a lot about a female by the way she dressed. She wore a plaid skirt, sleeveless blouse with the top two buttons undone and four-inch open-toed spikes and was giving out more signals than a Bridgeport hooker as she talked on her cell phone in front of her sparkling blue Lexus, her head tilted, her long auburn hair spilling over her shoulder.

She was great-looking for forty, her figure lean and toned. From what he heard, she played tennis and worked out at a spa in St. Clairsville, where she lived.

Ralph admired women who took care of themselves. Nadie had been a runner when she was a kid, even jogged in college, but stopped altogether during the last year. Maybe she'd take it up again when she found out they'd be rich. He'd like that.

But he had to be cool about this deal. Nadie was naïve, not stupid. The only thing keeping her from tossing him out was her forgiving heart—which she'd demonstrated frequently ever since he met her nearly six years earlier, when they were both taking courses at the local branch of Ohio U.

He was studying Business Management and had aspirations of starting up his own software company. He figured that with his drive and dedication, he might be able to get one off the ground in just a couple of years. It didn't take him long to realize how stupid he was.

His BM degree earned him a steady job at an advertising firm in Wheeling but didn't do much for his bank account. It was only when he met up with Maury, a childhood friend who had become a broker, that Ralph learned the proper way to achieve success.

Real estate was the answer. "You'll be rich before you know it," Maury had told him. "And you'll be up to your chin in hot-looking babes. They go into real estate because they can be their own boss, because of the wads of cash to be made, and because they can pick and choose who they want to shack up with."

Ralph always had great luck with the ladies. With his little-boy good looks, impeccable taste in clothes and bright smile, he was sure to work his way up in no time.

Nadie was his first conquest—which fed his ego considerably. Nadie was the ultimate unattainable type. He'd always suspected there was some other guy in the picture but later ruled that out when he'd seen no evidence of any sort of soured relationship. He then decided Nadie had had a bad experience in high school and was reluctant to make another mistake with the wrong guy.

In those days she was a doctor's assistant. She'd always wanted to study medicine in California but when her parents died, she missed her chance. And when the doctor she'd been working for died, things quickly went downhill.

The fact that she couldn't find another doctor to work for in Barnes made life difficult. Ralph wanted to sell the house and move to Pittsburgh for more opportunities, but she refused to leave Barnes. This was a low blow for Ralph, who thought his wife should go to the ends of the earth for him. And since she'd wanted to move to California from the beginning, he often wondered why she'd changed her mind. Pennsylvania was by no means California, but Pittsburgh was a stone's throw from Barnes and there were some good medical schools in the area, so he didn't see a problem. But Nadie was stubborn, and despite several attempts on his part to convince her to leave, she remained committed in her decision to stay.

Out of sheer frustration, Ralph left to make his own fortune. He hoped that without his financial support, Nadie would *have* to sell the house. When he returned, she'd leap into his arms and come to terms with what had to be done.

But he quickly found that she was still hanging on to her silly dreams.

He tried it again, this time shooting for Columbus, but despite a few promising prospects, his plans went bust. He returned to Barnes and toughed it out for six months, commuting the thirty-six miles to Wheeling for a boring office job that barely paid for the suit he'd bought for the occasion.

He left again, this time for Cincinnati, and came back in two months. And again five months later, heading back to Pittsburgh and returning in four.

When he returned five days ago after his latest disappointing venture, Nadie was still working at the local Five'n Dime. She even had some medical problem she wanted to discuss with him—no doubt brought on by nerves. He decided that this might be the perfect time to make her realize what they had to do.

The Country Club deal was bound to make good money. If he could get Nadie to agree, he could put up their house as collateral for a much larger project he had in the works.

But when he learned about Monty Niemus' Elm Street project, things quickly changed. Ralph's long- awaited success had finally come.

All he had to do was convince Nadie to sell.

But first he had to seal the deal with Rachel Hayworth. Using the money from the sale of Nadie's house would not only take care of Monty's money scheme, it would also give Ralph what he needed to get in with the Country Club crowd. That meant contacts a man could only dream about.

"You must be Ralph." Rachel pocketed her cell phone and gave him a warm smile. Her hand was small and cold. He often wondered why a woman's hands lacked warmth. He figured it was because she was nervous in the presence of a good-looking man.

"In the flesh," he said, staring into her large almond eyes and giving her The Grin.

Her smile lingered. And when she flicked some hair away from her cheek, he knew she was flirting with him. "We certainly picked a beautiful day for coming out here."

"Yes we did."

He followed her up the paved winding drive, where the L-shaped four-bedroom two-story brick with its two-car garage sat comfortably behind a freshly painted white picket fence and neatly trimmed bushes. "It's a really nice place," he said.

She unlocked the front gate and led the way down the stone walk. "It's dated, of course. The roof needs replaced, and there are issues with leakages and energy loss—"

"What's it been appraised for?"

"Four-fifty, but the asking price is four-oh-five. I've been told the owner's motivated and might come down another twenty."

"Sounds reasonable. How about we take a tour through the house, then talk about it over lunch?"

She stopped walking. "Lunch?"

"Lunch. You know. A restaurant. A nice, quiet booth. Food? A good wine? Lots of pleasant conversation?"

"Sounds lovely. Won't your wife mind?"

Ralph flashed another bright grin. "My wife is probably the most open-minded lady you'll ever want to meet."

CHAPTER 6

Rand and Harriet left the church and headed south through the thin alleyway separating the Barnes Savings & Loan and the First National Bank.

Squat brick and block buildings lined Main Street. The business district consisted of two blocks of shops. On the north side of Main Street, spanning east to west, the Barnes Corner Newsstand started the chain, which included the Barnes Café, Guidry's Meats, the East Main Laun-Dro-Matic, Clancy's Coffeehouse, Bob's Brush Cuts, Otto's Odds & Ends, Barnes Savings & Loan, and First National Bank. Bailey's Five'n Dime anchored the intersection on the other side of Chestnut, which divided East Main from West Main.

On the south side of Main, the Barnes 7-Eleven anchored the block from the east. The Barnes Drugstore continued the chain, including Lois's Flowers, Barney's Spirits Emporium, Lenny's Feed & Supply, Gary's Guns & Knives, Natalie's Nails, and Thompson Hardware, with Mark's Garage & Auto Body Shop across the street and directly south of the Five'n Dime.

The town had hardly changed. Rand had the strange feeling he hadn't moved away at all.

Harriet's voice startled him, but when he spun around to look at her, he noticed that her lips weren't moving.

"Too many others are about, so talk to me through your mind. Otherwise, they'll think you're crazy."

"But I *am* crazy," he whispered.

"Must you be a problem? Just do as I say."

"How's this?"

"Perfect."

She sighed. *"Was that so hard?"*

"I like the way your eyes bulge and quiver when I get you going."

"You're such a mess. In fact—" She stopped, placed the tips of her index fingers to her temples and closed her eyes. After about ten seconds she opened her eyes. *"That woman over there."*

Across the street at the corner, a well-dressed woman with thick brown hair paced in front of Thompson's Hardware. She consulted her wristwatch, then peered up and down the street.

"What about her?"

"She's about to have an accident."

"What?"

"An accident. You know. When something happens that isn't—"

"I know what an accident is. I meant, please explain."

"She's waiting for someone who's obviously very late. She thinks she's been stood up. Very shortly she'll cross the street in a huff. An idiot in a sports car will slam into her before she can get safely across. The idiot's had a few. He's returning to work late and is too buzzed to care what he's doing."

"How do you know all that?"

"Intuition."

"Can't you stop it?"

"My intuition?"

"The accident."

"No."

"Because it's her time?"

"It's not her time."

"Don't follow."

"If it was her time, I wouldn't get a premonition."

"Then you can save her."

"Not supposed to."

"You mean you're gonna let this woman die*?"*

"I'm not allowed to intervene," Harriet said.

Incredible. Were they supposed to stand around like morons while the poor woman got smeared?

"Listen, if you know something's about to—"

"It's out of my hands."

"What's that *supposed to mean?"*

"I can't save her...but you *can."*

The woman edged closer to the curb.

"Me?"

"You."

"Are you sure?"

"I believe this will be your first official job as my apprentice."

"Just what am I supposed to do?"

"Use your imagination."

"Can I fly yet? Maybe I can just fly on over there and—"

52

"And what? Scoop her up and set her down safely on the sidewalk?"

"It always worked for Superman."

"Rand, Superman's —"

"I know. A movie. Several movies, actually. And a comic strip character. It's also a really popular costume for trick-or-treaters."

"First of all, you can't fly—not without my help. Secondly, what will you tell her after you put her down?"

"I can't very well tell her I'm Superman—not in this outfit. Clark Kent dresses better."

"You're running out of time."

A distant roar shattered the silence.

"Harriet..." A cold shiver sliced through him.

"Could you use a helpful hint?"

"That would be nice..."

"But just this once, and only because you're new at this."

"Fine. Tell me..."

"You were something of a ladies' man not so very long ago, weren't you?"

"When I was much younger and a lot dumber."

The woman took another step closer to the curb.

"Do something ladies'-mannish."

It told him nothing. He didn't even know if there *was* such a phrase. Even if there was, it meant nothing to him right now, and even if it did he couldn't see how anything short of magic could save the woman from being run over.

"Harriet?"

She'd disappeared. The roar grew louder.

***

Frieda's mood over the last thirty seconds had progressed from mild irritation to a burning mad. One of those seething episodes that could make a girl unattractive if she didn't watch herself.

Temper, temper... Age lines, Frieda. Wrinkles. The bane of the sophisticated woman. Above all, flaws. God forbid any man should see a flaw on his goddess...

Here she was, finished with her manicure and pedicure and ready for the elegant lunch Edmund had promised her at the Café *Normandie* in Wheeling—and no sign of that stupid Olds anywhere...

No reason a woman of her breeding should have to wait at a street corner. Such a sight might conjure up improper thoughts. Since she owned a condo out near the country club, not many of these locals knew her. How could they possibly know she had money of her own and had run an employment agency in Wheeling nearly ten years?

But they knew her at the First National Bank across the street, where she kept one of her checking accounts. Since the batteries on her cursed cell had died, she could use one of their phones. Going back to Natalie's wouldn't be bright. Calling Edmund to find out what the holdup was would probably heat up quickly; she didn't want to become the salon's primary source of entertainment or gossip.

I won't forget, Edmund had promised. *Pick you up at twelve sharp.*

Well, it was now twelve-*thirty-eight*, and that vintage Oldsmobile still wasn't anywhere near camera range.

She approached the curb. She'd use a phone at the bank and let him know just how considerate and selfish—

Temper, temper...

A man rushed across the street in her direction, an urgency on his face one could easily interpret as fear.

What was he afraid of?

Nothing out of the ordinary behind her, or at the garage across the street.

As he drew closer, his fear vanished. What remained was a face that was very easy to look at.

His clothes left much to be desired. He'd either picked them up right off the floor or slept in them. The jacket and jeans were etched in deep fanlike wrinkles.

But judging by his long, easy strides, he was in good shape. His hair—unkempt, windblown, and in need of professional assistance—gave him a distinctive macho appearance.

Frieda knew she'd ever seen him before.

He stepped up to the curb and flashed a bright smile, igniting a high-octane glimmer in his large dark-brown eyes.

A loud, noxious roar erupted behind him. Running the red light at the intersection, a big muscle car whizzed by—one of those nasty-looking things with a stupid oblong box stuck in the middle of the long, sloped hood.

Frieda couldn't believe it. Speed limit was twenty— and the idiot had gone through red. A shame some people were so stupid.

A second sooner, this fox of a guy might have been run over.

"May I help you?" she asked.

"Sorry, thought you were someone else."

She turned on her best smile. Being over forty no longer bothered her. Thanks to that facelift she'd had last year, and the work done to zap those hideous crow's feet, she looked ten years younger than the DOB printed much too visibly on her driver's license. When you were the proud owner of a dazzling drop-dead smile, age rarely entered into the equation.

"Who were you looking for?" she asked.

"No one in particular. You just reminded me of some- one."

She wanted to ask more questions, keep the conversation going. She liked the man's eyes and smile. But her practical side—on cue, as always— made an irritating entrance. Pretty eyes notwithstanding, this man didn't appear prosperous enough to buy her a bagel and coffee.

But maybe if she found out a few details, the rest would fall into place. "You live in town?"

"I've been living in Orlando the last fifteen years."

Back then Frieda was living in a trailer park in St. Clairsville with her second husband, who'd convinced her that his success in business would take a second seat to his drinking and that awful cocaine habit he'd acquired less than a year after their wedding. Needless to say, his business career was a giant bust. So was the marriage.

"I wasn't here then."

"You were probably in high school," the handsome stranger said.

When was the last time a man had pressed that button? Not Edmund, certainly. His reputation and success in medicine were much too sophisticated to waste on such annoying trivialities as compliments, or the pressing of certain crucial buttons.

But a lady required constant attention, and some men just weren't equipped to deal with it. It was so very sad that the compliments all but vanished once a woman reached thirty-five.

"That's *so* sweet of you." Clothing really didn't matter all *that* much, did it? What mattered was what was what inside this person. And what she saw inside *this* person was absolute quality.

The black Olds roared up to the curb and stopped abruptly, rocking on ancient springs. Edmund and his horrible timing... "I...have to go," she heard herself saying.

"C'mon, Freed." Edmund rolled down the window, his heavy-featured face having that same frantic lost look all doctors wear when out of the office. "Gotta do the fast burger bit. I've got a pregnancy at one-fifteen, and I have to zip back."

"You're late," she snapped. "And you promised me lunch—not a *fast burger*."

Edmund's face paled. "I couldn't help it. This just came up..."

Frieda spun around on her heel. Maybe this guy with the dazzling smile would—

She was staring at her own puzzled reflection in the hardware store window.

CHAPTER 7

Feeling much better after her cry, Nadine went back to her register and rang up Mr. Schildmyer, the little man with the bottle-cap glasses who'd taught her Social Studies in high school.

"Thanks, Nadie." He scooped up his bag, which contained a bottle of Milk of Magnesia, a giant jar of Tums, and a pack of Puffs Ultra. "You're looking well, by the way. Still as slender as ever."

Funny how little she paid attention to her appearance nowadays. These days she checked her makeup to see that it looked presentable and her hair to make sure it wasn't too wild. Other than that, she no longer cared—at least, not as much as she did years ago. "I didn't think anyone noticed," she said, hoping she didn't sound angry or bitter.

"Actually, you look even better than when you were a student." He lowered his voice—as if they were sharing a dreadful secret. "Personally, I always thought you were a tad…skinny."

"I was really active back then. Running everywhere, climbing trees." Talking about it made it sound like it had happened in another life. To a little girl who thought—as well as hoped—life would always be exciting and fun.

"Well, it sure did you a lot of good," Mr. Schildmyer said.

"Thank you." She knew he was just being nice, but it made her feel better. Mr. Schildmyer was a sweet man. "I take it you're still at the school."

59

"How could you tell?"

She pointed to his bag.

He laughed and continued laughing even as he left the store.

She picked up her cell and tried the house again. No answer. She tried Ralph's cell. It went directly to voice mail.

So much for talking to the man. He was probably wining and dining his latest "venture."

The fact that he was with another woman didn't bother her as much as it should. She discovered a while ago that she no longer had the same feelings for Ralph. She supposed it had a lot to do with his leaving so much, but she wasn't even sure about that. She didn't love him as much as she wanted to, and this bothered her. She had a lot of love in her heart to give to someone. Most of it was unused stuff she hadn't displayed since she was much younger. She'd wanted to give it all to Ralph, to share a life with him and all the perks that came with being married. But his commitment to his career had taken precedence, and nothing else seemed to matter.

Not even her health.

Monty Niemus, dandy as ever in his expensive blue silk Italian suit, pushed his large square frame through the glass door. A beaming grin covered his plump, closely shaven cheeks. His glistening white Cadillac waited at the curb directly in front of the store.

"Hi, Nadie. I thought I'd drop by and see if we might be able to talk after you get off work."

"What about?"

"Your husband." The grin vanished—not a good thing.

"What…about him?"

Monty took a breath. "He stopped by my office to discuss a personal matter."

"What sort of personal matter?"

"Your house."

She didn't like the sound of this at all. "What about my house?"

Monty moved closer. No one was within earshot, but he lowered his voice anyway. This frightened her even more. "He stopped by to discuss selling me your house."

"Selling my *house*?"

Monty didn't reply; his expression remained grave.

"Monty, I think you're right. We do need to talk."

"When do you get off?"

"Six o'clock."

"Is the Barnes Café all right?"

"I'll meet you there."

CHAPTER 8

As Rand and Harriet waited in the alley for the classic Olds to pull away from the curb, Rand thought it funny that some of his old habits would serve him in the spirit world.

But there was no way he could have prepared for something like this. Most everyone feared death and avoided thinking about it. Contemplating one's usefulness in the hereafter is not common practice.

Women dominated the software profession. They started up companies, organized and ran them. They'd become an integral part of the computer age. Over the years their numbers had reached staggering proportions.

They were intelligent and resourceful. They were also outspoken and brazen. Beautiful but hard. Sexy but independent. You won't get far in business by being timid or submissive. And you won't advance by taking sexy suggestions to heart.

Business ethics had progressed over the years, evolving into a state of consensual flirtation. Office behavior was now synonymous with "people skills." Companies financing in-house classes encouraged their employees to improve themselves in this area.

Flirting had always been natural for Rand. It was harmless fun and struck up numerous friendships. However, this was the first time he'd ever used his skills to save a woman's life.

But as the Olds pulled away, he knew he'd somehow screwed up in his first job as Harriet's apprentice. The hazy red aura emanating from her white form was a dead giveaway.

"Something's wrong, isn't it?" he asked.

"How can you tell?"

"The fireball coming out of the top of your head has given me the tiniest clue."

"I have *been saying you're observant, haven't I?"*

"A blind man would notice that inferno. So...what's wrong?"

"As if you didn't know." She went back to watching the traffic.

"You told me to save the woman's life. I saved her, so there shouldn't be a problem, right?"

"Right."

"But there's obviously a problem."

"You were flirting."

"You told me to be 'ladies' mannish.'"

Harriet's arms were crossed in front of her. The red haze had thinned a little. *"You stayed right there, smiling and being cute. You should've gone on your merry way right after you said, 'I thought you were someone else.'"*

"That would've been rude. The woman was upset, wanted company."

"She wanted her boyfriend to pick her up."

"Like I said, it would've been rude."

"You were probably in high school?" Her deep sigh made him feel genuinely stupid. *"The woman's fifty if she's a day."*

"Women don't like to be reminded of their age."

"So lying works?"

"With a woman's age? You bet."

"Is that how you used to snare them?"

"You make it sound like I used a net."

"You didn't need one—not with those lies."

"Now you're being insulting."

"By calling it as I see it?"

"Sometimes women want to hear lies."

"I'll bet it usually worked."

"Most of the time."

"Not always?"

"Some women are impossible."

"Oh? What are we talking about now?"

"Impossible women. Like you."

"I'm impossible because I don't like lies?"

He had a strong feeling he should end this quickly. *"Women need to be appreciated."*

"Of course. What was I thinking?"

Now she was humoring him. She looked bored, for one thing. She even raised a hand, presumably to stifle a yawn. She was probably just trying to needle him by being a nag.

"You think I'm a nag?"

"Dandy." Now he wanted to vanish. *"She walks through walls, sets her fingers on fire, and reads minds."*

"Mind-reading's easy when we're talking like this. Our thoughts get mixed in with our words. How am I a nag?"

"You're not."

"Why say it, then?"

"I was just venting."

She said nothing. The red aura had disappeared.

"Have we finished arguing?" he asked.

"I guess..."

"You sound disappointed."

"Could be..."

"Yep. Impossible, all right."

They crossed the street with the light.

A short, plump woman left Guidry's Meats. She was carrying a large stack of brown bundles and was having difficulty managing the step down to the sidewalk. Her heel twisted. Just as she was about to go down, Rand saw himself grabbing her and holding her up while she corrected her footing. When she'd recovered, she looked down at her feet to figure out what just happened.

"Did you do that?" Harriet asked.

"I'm not sure."

"Tell me what happened."

"I visualized myself grabbing her while she got her foot under her again."

"You did it, then."

"How come I couldn't do that with the woman at the curb?"

"You were too busy being nervous and flustered. And, of course, thinking of Superman."

"Wow. Dead just a short time and I already have powers?"

"You'll find them developing constantly."

"Cool."

"Just don't go overboard."

"Of course not." This was great. It was just like *Bishop's Wife.*

Down the street, a bald man around sixty-five or so was fighting with the newspaper box, punching it, shaking it, and yelling at it. It wouldn't open.

Rand thought, *Open sesame.*

The door suddenly dropped open.

The man snatched up his paper, slammed the box shut and stomped away.

"Why did you do that?" Harriet sounded more angry than curious.

"For two reasons. First of all, because that's happened to me, and when it did, I wanted to be able to work some magic. Junk food machines are next on my list."

"I can't wait. And what's the second reason?"

"Because I can."

"Did you hear me less than twenty seconds ago when I told you not to go overboard? Or weren't you paying attention?"

"I heard you."

"Good. You have to keep yourself in check. You're not supposed to use your new powers at the drop of a hat, you know. If you're not careful, it can backfire on you."

"How?"

"Take my word for it, all right?"

"But it's so much fun. And you keep saying this is supposed to be fun, right?"

Harriet rubbed her eyes. *"I've created a monster."*

"I'll use my powers only to do good," he said, standing tall and proud. *"For truth, justice, and the American way."*

Harriet sighed. *"Will you* please *stop with the Superman stuff?"* She started walking again.

He caught up. *"I've got a question that's been bugging me."*

"Maybe I'll have an answer for you."

"That nasty deal you pulled a couple of minutes ago. With the woman at the curb."

She blinked. *"What nasty deal?"*

"Disappearing."

"It worked, didn't it? Made you think for yourself."

"Didn't have much choice, did I?"

"If I'd dallied a moment longer, the woman would be dead."

Halfway down the block, the big painted sign above Clancy's Coffeehouse, faded and chipped from age and the elements, swayed in the breeze. The heavy aromas of crispy bacon, hash brown potatoes, and strong chicory coffee drifted their way.

"How about some coffee?" he asked. *"I could go for a cup."*

"Maybe later."

"I used to go there all the time when I lived here. Besides, it'll just take a few minutes."

"Later. Things to do, people to help."

"I can't go on saving lives and helping people without coffee."

Harriet sighed deeply. *"They didn't tell me you'd be* this *difficult..."*

"What did *they say?"*

"Just that you were a hard case."

67

"You sure you haven't been talking to my mother?"

"Why would you think of her?"

"That sounds like something she'd say."

"I think the term fits."

"I wonder who else up there has got a hard-on against me."

"We don't call them that."

"What do you call them?"

"Issues. Concerns."

"Hmmm...Heaven sounds corporate."

"Watch your language."

"Sorry."

"We don't have too many CEO's up there at all."

"What about lawyers?"

She flinched; he'd obviously struck a nerve. *"It's called Heaven for a reason."*

"Yep. Sounds like a pretty cool place."

"I'm glad you approve."

"Right now I've got to, don't I? I'm just your ordinary dead guy in really tacky clothes."

"Why so down on yourself?"

"Because I'm dead—why else?"

"It happens to everyone."

"Yeah. The very last *thing."*

"How can you say that? Look around. You're still here. The only difference is you've lost your body."

"A shame, too. I took care of it. Worked out, watched what I ate, and didn't go overboard on the booze."

"Things really aren't so bad, are they?"

"Could be worse, I guess. I always worried about dying. Now I don't have to."

"It's just a change no one understands until it actually happens."

The sun had swooped down in the west, dimming the afternoon in a translucent cloak of dark blue.

"What happened to the lunch hour?" Strange how quickly the sky had darkened. It seemed like just a few minutes had passed since his encounter with the woman at the curb.

"Time slows down only when there's something for us to do."

Someone bumped into Rand.

"Excuse me," said a husky female voice close to his ear.

A whiff of lavender. A twinge of memory.

His head grew hot. The large, long-lashed blue eyes held his before shifting to the brick building in front of them, then back to him, lingering one last delicious moment.

No. It can't *be.* He backed up and let her pass. Another whiff of lavender caressed him.

The passing traffic diminished in volume, then faded. The air grew warm and hazy. A giant bubble encased him.

Nothing existed but the beautiful blonde slipping through the wide doorway of the restaurant.

CHAPTER 9

Confident the day was turning out well, Ralph ordered another round of martinis while Rachel made her trip to the ladies room.

On the other side of the large, tinted window, the front lot of the La-Z Inn was nearly deserted. In a few hours the place would be hectic with businessmen en route to Columbus or Pittsburgh. The bar would be jumping with travelers and swingers from St. Clairsville looking for fresh meat.

He was confident Rachel liked him. She'd bumped against him several times when she was showing him the house—a sure sign. If he'd learned one thing about women, it was that they didn't get too close when they weren't interested.

But he could tell she wasn't a pushover. Her outfit, jewelry, and new Lexus said she was bright, knew what she was doing and wasn't about to risk her reputation just because she liked the way a man looked. The fact that she was divorced three times was testament to her independent spirit.

She liked to flirt and have a good time, but her main concern was getting the best price she could for the house. That was her business.

Ten minutes later, Rachel returned from the ladies room.

"Everything okay?" he asked. "All the parts still working?"

"All *too* well." She'd brushed her hair, repaired her makeup, and applied more gingery perfume. She climbed the stool next to him just as the waiter gave them fresh drinks. "Trying to get me drunk?"

"Maybe. Problem?"

She lifted her glass. "One more of these and driving home will no longer be an option."

"That makes two of us. Whaddya think we should do about that?"

She set her glass down. "Personally, I don't think driving home would be smart. I've heard about the cops in this town."

"And the cops in St. Clairsville are much more laid-back?"

She laughed. "You've got a point there."

"So how do I stand with this flip?"

"Like I told you before, the down payment is the last word."

"Yeah. Ten percent."

"Good memory."

"That's around forty K."

"Good at math, too."

He sipped his drink. Forty K. A tidy sum—especially when you didn't have it.

"Problem?"

"Maybe, maybe not." He didn't want her to think he had nothing going for him, so he gave her a quick version of The Grin. One thing he'd learned about wheeling and dealing was that you never let the opposition know your situation—or your weaknesses.

71

She shifted on her stool, moving closer and sending more ginger his way. "I've already told you. There's another prospective buyer in the pic."

"I know."

"This buyer's got cash."

"I think I might be able to make this worth your while."

"I'm listening."

"But I will need you to do me a teensy favor."

"Go on."

"Tell this prospective buyer the place has already been sold."

"No can do."

"Why not?"

"It's unethical. Unprofessional, at best."

"I really *want* the place—"

"You have the money?"

"It'll be a little while before I can get it."

She sighed. "How *much* of a little while?"

"Three days?"

She shook her head. "*Two* days…"

He just sighed.

"Ralph, the other guy has the money *now*."

She was being stubborn. He knew then that he was going to have to use more of his charm and people skills. "What can I do…to make you change your mind?"

"Depends."

"On what?"

"On what you've got for a teaser."

"I've got a house worth a hundred grand."

"And?"

"All I have to do is get the owner to sign it over."

She pushed a handful of hair away from her face. "Ralph, no one is going to—"

"Give me a day, all right? Two days, tops."

"I don't know…"

He placed his hand on top of hers.

She looked at it. "What else have you got?"

With his other hand, he reached into his pocket, pulled out the room key and dropped it on the counter between their drinks.

"It's getting a *little* better."

"Just a *little*?"

Her eyes were still fixed on the key. "Let's just say I'm willing to examine your methods of persuasion."

CHAPTER 10

Nadine paused in the cool, dark foyer of the Cafe.

There was something about that guy she'd bumped into. It was strange…almost like she'd seen him before, had known him somewhere…

What was it? His smell? His eyes?

They were nice eyes. A soft brown…and they seemed to sparkle. They held you fast, made you feel helpless and warm.

When was the last time she'd felt that way? A *very* long time ago.

Enough of that. Focus on the talk with Monty. About Ralph. And the house. *Her* house. The place she loved.

The home Ralph wanted to take away from her.

The mortgage was in her name only. Ralph couldn't do anything to sell the house from under her.

Legally, that is.

So why was she so worried about it?

Maybe it was because Ralph had gone to Monty to discuss it, and everyone knew Monty wasn't the most reputable businessman in town. Monty schemed. And made acquisitions. And bargained. And set traps. Monty did whatever was necessary to get what he wanted.

And it was common knowledge that he wanted Nadine's house.

So what was this all about?

The dark candlelit room hummed with the sounds of soft music, whispering, subdued laughter and the light tingling of silverware.

The Café had been a Barnes institution more than forty years. She'd come here many times, with her parents and sisters years ago, most recently with Ralph, and by herself. It provided the perfect atmosphere for relaxation, especially when you wanted to be pampered.

But this time there would be no pampering. No relaxation or other pleasantries. Monty was going to talk about his discussion with Ralph—which would ultimately lead to the foreclosure. But her health problem would, as always, take precedence in her mind, making her want to crumble—as she'd wanted to do more and more lately.

Why couldn't you fade away when you wanted to?

When you finished reading a book, you put it back on the shelf or gave it to a friend. When a program ended, another one came on. If you didn't like the show, you switched the channel. Why couldn't you do the same when your life grew intolerable?

She wanted to click her fingers and transport herself to a tropical island, surrounded by tanned, sarong-clad servants giving her backrubs and pina coladas.

Most of all, she wanted to do something— *any*thing— that would make the hurting stop.

Monty hunched over a glass of red wine at a small round table in a secluded corner of the room.

A full glass occupied the center of the setting opposite him.

Behind him, the mural of a forest overlooking a small lake embellished the stucco wall. The scene appeared unnaturally real in the flickering candlelight. The shadows could have been made by a nearby campfire.

Despite her reluctance, Nadine was drawn toward the mural.

"I hope I wasn't being presumptuous." Monty's small dark eyes flickered in the candlelight. "I thought you might enjoy a glass of port."

"I probably need one." She appreciated the gesture but wondered if she should have any. Lunch had been a cup of coffee. Breakfast, coffee, and a piece of buttered toast. But the wine might mellow her. Or take some of the bite out of the hurt she was experiencing from what Ralph was trying to do. And from her test results. "How is it?"

"Very good." It was also strong. She'd never been able to drink very much and would most likely be unable to finish. She didn't think it would be very bright to attempt a full glass. Monty had already finished his and was pouring more from the bottle near his elbow.

"This is a great place, isn't it?" he said.

"I've always loved it." The scampi had been her favorite since Momma first offered her one when Nadine was little. They really knew how to prepare it here.

76

She had another tiny swallow of the port. Monty lifted the bottle and dropped another inch into her glass just as she put it back down.

"Tell me what Ralph said." It was time to get to the main issue.

"He told me he could give me your house."

"As easy as that?"

Monty shrugged. "He made it sound as if the deal was already in the can."

She wanted to find him and scratch his eyes out. But her only reaction was to raise the glass to her lips.

"Might I ask a personal question?" he asked. "About the house?"

"Sure."

"How'd you get so far behind? Was it the insurance premiums? They've been increasing steadily the last couple of years."

"Nearly double since I first bought the place. Unfortunately, my paycheck hasn't been able to keep up. When I bought the house Ralph was working in Wheeling and I was a doctor's assistant."

"I remember. Then Ralph left. Pittsburgh, wasn't it?"

"Which time?" She tried to smile but her facial features suddenly felt unnaturally heavy.

Monty didn't reply.

"When Doc Adams died, I couldn't get the same type of job. I eventually ran out of time and had to settle for the Five'n Dime, which pays much less than what I was making before."

"And you've been getting behind ever since."

"The past year has been really tight."

"Ralph hasn't helped, I take it."

The heat came back and settled near the base of her neck. "I just can't believe he told you he'd sell it—"

"He can't. His name isn't on the title."

"Thank God it's my house. I may be behind in the mortgage payments, but it's all mine. For now, anyway."

"I'll bet Abner's putting the pressure on."

"Mr. Hargrove's a very nice man. He's got no choice. I'm three payments behind." She picked up her wine glass. She was already feeling the effects but had another small sip anyway. Talking about this was upsetting.

The waiter appeared with the menus. Monty reached into his jacket pocket for his reading glasses. "How's the scampi, Al?"

"Just got in a fresh shipment of gulf shrimp this morning, Mr. Niemus," the waiter replied.

Nadine couldn't help wondering if Monty was a mind-reader.

"Good batch?"

"The best."

"And the prime rib?"

"Just the way you like it."

Monty lowered his menu. "How about it, Nadie?"

"How'd you know?"

He chuckled. "I've been in this restaurant a dozen times while you were here, and you've always

78

ordered the scampi. I mean always. It doesn't take a rocket scientist."

"I really don't know," she said. This wasn't supposed to be a dinner date.

"Aren't you hungry?"

"I'm upset."

"Give us a few minutes," Monty told Al, who bowed dutifully and slipped away.

Nadine just couldn't focus on food. She picked up her wine glass. Ignoring the growing warmth, she coaxed another minuscule spoonful into her throat.

"Ralph has some sort of scheme."

"I know."

"He wants to use your house to finance whatever he's working on."

She nodded.

"Why would he even try something like this?"

"You don't know?"

"How would I?"

"I thought maybe he'd try convincing *you* to do something."

"Like what?"

She wanted Monty to know she was suspicious but didn't want him to think she considered him the bad guy in this situation. If Monty was scheming with Ralph, he wouldn't have told her about this in the first place.

"I have no idea," she said subtly. "I really don't know him anymore. Every time he comes back home, he's different. I don't know if it's the strain of constant failure or the stress. He doesn't even look at me the same anymore."

"I might have a way to help you out."

She found herself growing suspicious again. Monty might have given her a heads-up about Ralph's scheme, but some things just couldn't be ignored. Monty owned businesses, rental properties, private residences. He lived in a mansion, kept a fleet of classic cars and had a fifty-foot yacht. He owned just about everything.

His grin told her he knew what she was thinking. "You're skeptical."

"Yes."

"I've known you since high school. Friends help out one another, don't they?"

She'd never considered Monty a friend. He'd been after her since her senior year when she'd gone out for track. Monty was busy starting up his business ventures then, but he always showed up at football games and track and field events. He'd never been subtle about his intentions. The flirting hadn't stopped even after his marriage to Nancy.

"What about the Elm Street project?" she asked.

"What about it?"

"You need my house for that, don't you?"

"Not necessarily."

Was this the truth? She couldn't tell. The man was shrewd—there was no way he was going to let anyone know what he was planning.

"You mean—"

"I can make that deal happen even without your house."

"But all I've been hearing is that—"

"People love talking about things they know nothing about."

"What are you saying? The project—"

"The project will go with or without your house. You can stay there as long as you wish."

"But what about the mortgage? Mr. Hargrove can't possibly let this go."

"I'll make a couple of phone calls."

"To who?"

"All you need to know," he said softly, "is that you'll be able to keep your home."

"But how…I mean why…how can I possibly repay—"

"We'll talk about that later, all right?"

The room had grown warmer.

Monty began blending into the forest behind him. She watched numbly as he lifted the bottle again, refilling her glass. The rich maroon liquid winked at her in the candlelight, telling her everything would be just fine.

Just then, everything began to dim.

"Nadie? You all right?"

CHAPTER 11

Rand pressed his back against the brick wall of the Barnes Café and stared straight ahead, at the 7-Eleven across the street. The people walking past immediately blurred into dark, hazy shapes.

"*Rand?*" Harriet's distant voice sounded muffled.

He didn't reply; his mind was in a loop. The accident. The wavy gobs in front of him turning into a slender figure in white. A body that wasn't even his own.

Now this.

Nadine, of all people. The last person he ever expected to see again.

"*Are you all right?*"

"*Are you serious?*" The heat erupted from him. It took all his strength to keep from shouting. "*Of course I'm not all right. I'm dead!*"

"*Besides that.*"

"*You mean being dead isn't bad enough?*"

Harriet was watching him curiously—possibly checking for signs of dementia. "*You were all right a minute ago.*"

"*I haven't been all right since I've met you.*"

Harriet's sapphire blues blazed. "*You don't have to be insulting.*"

"*Forgive me, okay? I'm falling apart here.*"

"*What's changed? You saved a woman's life and kept another from breaking her ankle. And don't forget your fearless newspaper caper.*"

"I wasn't all right..."

"You seemed to be."

"What can I say? I can put on a happy face with the best of them."

"It wasn't exactly a happy face."

"For me, that was a happy face."

"What's different?"

"I'm dead and have been walking around in someone else's body. That in itself should put me in a gnarly mood, wouldn't you say?"

"Tell me what's really bothering you…"

"Why don't I let you guess this time?"

"It was her, isn't it?"

He didn't reply. As usual, she was dead-on.

"The young woman you just bumped into. That was Nadine."

He tried to read her expression but couldn't see anything beyond the concern, the sincerity. *"How do you know about—"*

"I was told."

He wanted to ask how she knew but it didn't matter. The only thing that mattered was that Nadine was here. And after fifteen years, so was he.

"Tell me about it."

"You just said they told you everything."

"Tell me about Nadine. About you and her. And why your insides have suddenly turned into Jell-O."

Go ahead, tell her. It wouldn't hurt anything at this stage, would it? Water over the bridge. Besides, you're dead. Nothing can get to you now, right?

"This goes back to the old days."

"You were a musician back then."

83

"I'd had a big dose of the spotlight. It spoils you, shields you from reality. It gives you the illusion you're something more than the average guy. When it ends and the lights are turned off, you climb down from the stage. The audience is gone. You're all by yourself in the darkness. The applause, the excitement, the laughter—everything has disappeared. You want it to come back but know it never will. Your whole life changes. Your self-image has also dimmed, and you've become just another guy with bills to pay. Everything else has turned into filler for your memory banks.

"Our band broke up and I knew I had to find another profession. Synthesizers and RAP had taken over. Club owners no longer wanted to waste money on any other kinds of bands."

"Makes no sense."

"Club owners aren't exactly the brightest bulbs in the box. But since they're the ones paying, they've got the last word. The music field was changing, nonetheless. And since I was being squeezed out, I decided to make a clean break. Software looked promising, so I tried that."

"How'd you end up here?"

"One of our last gigs took place on a riverboat in Moundsville during prom season. This girl taught English at the local branch of Ohio U. She showed up on the riverboat as a chaperone and we hit it off. She lived in Barnes, so I started coming out to see her until our band broke up.

"Belmont Tech was offering computer courses and Ohio U was also busy with software classes.

The programs were much cheaper than the Pittsburgh schools, so that was another plus."

"What about this girl?"

"We broke up."

"How tragic." Harriet looked like she was about to cry.

"Want a Kleenex?"

"Don't need those anymore."

"Good. I don't have any. Even if I did, they'd be falling through the holes in the pockets of my custom Goodwill ensemble."

She ignored his comment. *"So I take it you stayed here because of your new career?"*

"It was commuting distance from Wheeling. I figured I could live here, finish my education and run a software business from Wheeling."

"Tell me about Nadine."

"She was an impressionable kid who lived two doors down from the apartment house I was renting. That house we passed on East Main. She saw me one day when I went to get a cheeseburger and fries at the Burger King. The way she stared at me told me she thought I was the greatest thing since sliced bread. At the time I needed that kind of boost. It was the same sort of hero worship I'd experienced as a musician, and it hit the spot during that time in my life. When a guy is idolized by a pretty young girl, life is great again."

The sun had already gone down, bringing about the first gray sprinkling of approaching dusk, although talking about Nadine had lightened his mood.

"Did you take advantage of the situation?"

"She was too young."

85

"How young?"

"She was fifteen then."

Harriet shrugged. *"That doesn't stop most men."*

"It stopped me."

"Why?"

"I was born with this killer conscience that would keep me awake nights. This good/bad, right/wrong morality mindset got hold of me early in life. They used to call me 'Mister Boy Scout' in high school because I had so many principles."

"You didn't like having them?"

"Sometimes they got in the way."

"You're saying you didn't want to have principles when Nadine came into your life?"

"Tough having principles when a pretty young blonde who thinks you're as fine as fox fur lives so close."

A vertical line appeared between her flaxen brows. *"We've got to spend time with her. She's in trouble."*

He stiffened. *"What...kind of trouble?"*

"Something must be done. And quickly."

"How can we help?"

"We've got to change a few things."

"You mean events*?"*

"Exactly."

"You're not talking about her past, are you?"

"We're not allowed to touch the past. That's taboo."

"Why?"

"You change the past, you also change the future."

"I know. Look at those Terminator *movies."*

"Just movies, dear. Very silly. If you really went back and killed someone before they were born, the entire future would be different."

"You've seen those flicks?"

"I saw the first one. It was more than enough."

"Didn't think too much of them?"

"Strictly for the mindless teen crowd."

"I take it you don't like teen slasher flicks, either."

"You're serious?"

"Sure. Let it out."

"Why should anyone with a brain cell like those?"

He grinned. *"I'm fond of them for the wet tee shirts."*

"Rand...those young women are so stupid..."

"I like that, too."

Harriet rubbed her temples. *"Sometimes you can be so male..."*

He wondered once again who she'd been talking to. *"Sounds like a lot of folks up there know me."*

"Could be. But like I said, we don't touch the past."

"Then we must be poking around with the future."

"We're not altering the future. We're tweaking a tiny sliver of the present. If something isn't adjusted very soon and certain elements are allowed to proceed, Nadine's future will be doomed."

"I don't understand."

"Nadine is the reason we've come to Barnes. I'm surprised you never suspected."

"I assumed she'd moved away. She wanted to study medicine so she could help people. She even mentioned California. I figured she'd do better in a much larger place."

"Well, she's still here. And you're the one who must save her."

"Will this be similar to what I did for that woman at the corner?"

"It'll be much more complicated. What she's going through is too much for her. If we leave things alone, she'll give up and the negative elements in her life will destroy her. If there's any way we can change her present situation, we must do it."

The prospect of approaching her, talking to her, looking into her eyes again, was too much. He knew he'd crumble. He'd come close to that only moments before, just by bumping into her. *"She'll remember me."*

"You're different, remember?"

"Not from where I sit."

"Rand, you're the only being in the Universe who can help her. This is a very traumatic period in her life. Helping someone in this situation is quite an honor. It's not yet her time. She needs you. If you don't step in, something horrible will happen."

Rand stumbled over to the park bench and dropped heavily onto its hard seat. He felt a hundred years old, every joint heavy and aching.

Harriet drifted over and joined him. *"She doesn't want to be with the man she's dining with. He's not a nice man."*

"What's she doing with him?"

"She's being told something she doesn't want to hear about her no- account husband. She's scared, and at a point in her life where nothing makes sense any more. She's about to lose her home."

"She's...got a husband?"

"It's not a happy marriage. It never was."

"It wasn't her fault. She had a lot of love to give."

"He wasn't the one who wanted it. But he isn't even her worst problem."

"There's more?"

"Just the other day she was told by her doctor that she is very sick."

A trickle of ice tapped him between the shoulder blades.

"How sick?"

"She's dying, Rand."

"My God. How can we possibly do anything to help her?"

Harriet's expression was grim. *"If we don't step in, the poor girl will die before tonight's end."*

CHAPTER 12

"I think I've had too much wine…"

Nadine slumped in her seat. The room shifted; the candles lighting the tables on her left skittered to the right, then ebbed back into stillness. The branches of the trees behind Monty swayed even though there was no wind.

"But you haven't even had that much…"

"Haven't had much…to eat…today." She groped for her purse. The growing nausea brought on a wave of dizziness. "I'm not a drinker, Monty. Never have been."

"Maybe after you've had some food…" He was standing, his right hand reaching for her.

"I…need to lie down." She pulled away. She didn't want him touching her. He was trying to help her but his touch made her cringe. She didn't want anyone invading her space right now.

Maybe she was just angry at everyone because she was so furious with Ralph.

"If there's anything I can do—"

"I'll be all right. Really. I just hope I can make it to my car—"

"You shouldn't drive home, feeling as you do. Let me take you."

"I…couldn't ask you to do that." But what choice did she have? Couldn't handle a car when she was feeling this way, could she? She'd never driven drunk before and didn't intend to start now.

Calling a cab made more sense.

"It's not a problem." Monty sounded upset. "After all, I'm the one who's been thoughtlessly refilling your glass."

"But—"

"No buts about it." He dug into a pocket, pulled out a thick wad of bills, then suddenly faded before her eyes, blending into the forest again...

Or maybe *she* was the one fading. Good. She'd wanted to turn the channel for some time. Close the book. Open the door. Evaporate. Get out.

She managed to stand. Now...if she could leave without falling on her face...

Push the chair gently back with your legs. Turn around slowly—no sudden moves. If you can stay on your feet, you'll make it outside in no time.

Maybe some fresh air...

***

The Cafe had hardly changed.

The same small square tables, candlelight, pillars and chandeliers, and ceramic tile floor. The stone fireplace separating the dining area and the dance floor was just as Rand remembered.

From the barstool he could see the reflection of Nadine's honey-blond hair in the bar mirror. She sat at a table in a dark corner, her back to him.

"Help you?" The stocky barman wore a bulldog-type scowl. He was checking out Rand's clothes—no doubt wondering if he had enough money for a drink.

"Waiting for someone, thanks."

"How 'bout a quick one while ya wait?"

"I'll let you know."

91

The barman swabbed down the polished counter near Rand's elbows. The blinking dark eyes clearly said: *I ain't too wild about freeloaders.* Without a word he rejoined the drinkers at the other end of the bar.

Nadine's dining companion advertised an expensive wardrobe and plenty of flashy jewelry. Broad and portly, he sported thick, shiny brown hair styled in a careful pompadour. He sat facing Nadine, picking up a wine bottle and topping off her glass as soon as she set it back down.

"Reminds me of Edward Arnold," he told Harriet, who sat perched on the bar counter beside him. *"Same clothes, same paunch, same hair."*

"Who?"

He frowned. *"Don't tell me you never heard of Edward Arnold."*

"The singer?"

"The movie actor."

"I thought he was a singer."

"There were two of them."

"Which one are you talking about?"

"The actor."

"Let me guess. Monty Niemus reminds you of Edward Arnold because of some movie."

"You catch on quick."

"I'm not just a pretty face. Which movie?"

"Diamond Jim."

"Never heard of it."

"You wouldn't."

"Don't be ugly. Just because I'm not obsessed with movies—"

"Diamond Jim was a weird millionaire."

"They call them eccentric when they're weird and rich."

"Why is that?"

Harriet shrugged. *"Anyone can be weird. When you're rich, the term weird just doesn't cut it. Don't you know the rich are different?"*

"I've heard that before. Anyway, Diamond Jim had a thing for money, food, and Lillian Russell."

"The actress?"

"You have been doing your homework."

"I thought Judge Roy Bean liked Lillian Russell."

"You're thinking of Lily Langtry."

Harriet shook her head. *"I seem to be getting my Lily's mixed up with my Lillian's…"*

Across the room, Monty Niemus dropped more wine into her glass.

Rand sat bolt upright. *"He's trying to get her drunk."*

"He plans to use her desperation for his own advantage."

"I take it he's trying to soften her up for something."

"I'm sure he knows exactly what he's doing."

Nadine shifted in her chair. She groped for her purse, nearly dropping it.

"His scheme worked. She's obviously had too much to drink."

Nadine stood, nearly losing her balance. Niemus slid out of the booth. He moved toward her, reaching out for her, but she pulled away. A waiter appeared. The two men helped her down the aisle.

"This is where you come in, Rand."

The white blur beside him dimmed into nothingness.

CHAPTER 13

Al stayed close to Nadine, watching her in case she stumbled. He had the same worried look all waiters had whenever a customer left with anything but a smile on their face.

"Should I call 911, Mr. Niemus?"

"Won't be necessary. I'll be taking her right home."

"What exactly happened? Is she sick?"

"The lady's had a long day, not much to eat. I should've thought of that before I refilled her glass—or at least asked."

Al, good soldier that he was, listened respectfully. "All she needs is rest."

Monty unlocked the passenger door and opened it. He was careful to get her in without her bumping her head. He was also careful to hide his irritation: he'd really been in the mood for their prime rib. He'd had no idea Nadine wouldn't be able to handle a glass or so of port wine.

But the evening wasn't a total loss. He was confident he'd convinced her she could keep her house. She'd start thinking about it once she sobered up and his plans for the Elm Street Project would begin.

"Sure you'll be all right, Mrs. Connelly?" Al watched as Monty strapped her in.

"I'm fine..." Her smile was more relaxed than usual. "Just really tired..."

"She's in good hands." Monty slid his hand into the side pocket of his creased slacks, peeled off a twenty from the wad and handed it over.

"*Thank* you, sir." Al trotted off happily.

Monty slid in behind the wheel. Beside him, Nadine squirmed in her seat. Her eyes were closed; her hair spilled over the shoulder strap of the seatbelt. He couldn't understand how a loser like Connelly could have snared such a doll. Why was it that the best babes always fell for the biggest duds?

The dash clock said 6:47. He needed a drink. A strong one. After he dropped off Nadine he could head on out to the La-Z Inn and have a couple of their excellent martinis. They always made them stronger than at the Café because of the heavy tourist trade they got out there. Their dining room would be open until eight; maybe he could have a bite there. Their prime rib was good, although not quite on the same scale as the Café's.

He flicked on the ignition.

A man in wrinkled clothes was standing directly in front of the Caddie, his hands buried in the pockets of his faded corduroys.

What the hell?

Monty waited. The man didn't budge. *Lovely.* He grabbed the gear shift, preparing to put it in reverse. A small pickup pulled in behind them. *Son of a bitch…*

The bum was now standing close to Monty's door. *I don't need this*, he thought, locking up. Bad enough his plans for the evening were shot. Now he had some weirdo keeping him from going anywhere. Probably looking for a handout.

The bum tapped on the window.

Monty pressed a button on the armrest. With a soft hum, the window eased down about four inches. "Problem?"

"Everything okay in there?"

"Why wouldn't it be?"

"Nadine looks drugged. Or dead."

"She's not dead, she's—you *know* Nadine?"

"Yes, I know her."

Of *course* she'd know a bum. Nadine knew everyone. She worked in the Five'n Dime, didn't she?

"How come she doesn't look fine?"

"Take my word for it. She's fine."

"Her eyes are closed. And her head's bobbing all over the place."

"She's tired. I'm taking her home."

"It's not even seven o'clock. She's too young to be this tired so early."

Damn. All he needed—a bum with irritating explanations.

"She's had a little too much wine."

"Nadine *drinks*?"

Monty sighed. This was grating on his last nerve. "No, she doesn't drink—"

"Then why'd she have too much wine?"

Monty's cheeks flushed. *Cool it. Don't forget the results of your last blood pressure exam.* "I gave her a little port."

97

"Why give her wine when you know she doesn't drink?"

"We were *talking*. I thought she might *like* a little port. We *were* in a restaurant, after all."

"But if you knew she doesn't drink—"

"Listen…I didn't know she hadn't had anything to eat. All right? Am I off the hook now?" *What the hell am I* doing? *I'm explaining myself to a* bum.

"So you're taking her home now?"

"That's what I said."

"I don't believe you."

"Let's touch base here, bub." He could sense his heart rate fluttering, the heat increasing around his collar. "This really isn't any of your business. Understand?"

Nadine shifted in the seat. "Who are you…talking to?"

"Nadine?" The bum rapped on the window.

Monty wanted to grab him by the neck and choke him.

No can do. Too public. Try another approach.

He shoved a fist down his trouser pocket. He didn't even bother to notice what was in his palm; it didn't matter. All he wanted was to get out of here. Since when did bums care about anything other than booze and a box to crash in?

"Buy yourself a nice big jug of Ripple." Monty pushed a bill through the crack.

"Nadine?" Ignoring the money, the bum circled the car and groped for the locked passenger door.

"Who…*is* that?" Nadine peered out her window.

"Nobody." The pounding in Monty's head drowned out everything. "Just sit back, I'll get you home in just— "

"Nadine!"

Monty jammed his foot down on the gas. Spinning tires, the Cadillac leaped from its spot and roared down Main Street.

***

Rand watched numbly as the Cadillac squealed to a stop at the end of the block, then turned right at the intersection.

"That went as well as expected." Harriet appeared at the curb, the folds of her white robe fluttering in the breeze.

It was difficult to control his anger. *"Did it again, didn't you?"* He glared at her, the frustration making his limbs shake.

"Did what *again?"* She seemed totally unaffected. She was staring back at him as if his sudden flare of emotion was strangely fascinating.

"You do a really lousy Claude Rains impersonation."

"Who?"

"Turning invisible at the most inopportune time. Instead of giving me some idea of what I'm supposed to do. Disappearing is so much easier than hanging around and being helpful."

"You've got to do this on your own. It's your mission. You're the only one who can help her."

"All I managed to do was piss Niemus off."

"In this case it might have been a good thing to stir the pot. You forced his hand."

99

"He's taking her home. How did I force his hand?"

Harriet blinked. *"I have a feeling he's not taking her home."*

"Where else would he be taking her?"

"What were you thinking when he told you he was taking her home?"

"I figured a jerk like him would want to take her to a motel. Now that you've mentioned it, I did catch an image of the La-Z Inn off I-70 intermingling with his thoughts."

"Oh boy..."

"What's that supposed to mean?"

"You might have influenced his plans for the evening."

Her inference caused a jolt of heat racing down his spine.

"You don't think he actually caught what I was thinking, do you?"

"I told you to be careful for a reason. Remember what I said about a backfire?"

"You mean—"

"Exactly. You implanted the idea in his head."

"Can I... do that?"

"You just did."

"I'm getting pissed off again."

"Why are men so emotional in a crisis?"

"We don't call it that."

"What do you call it?"

"Being macho."

"That's just another word for stupid."

"Whatever. But since you brought it up, any ideas?"

"You're asking a mere woman *what to do in your present state of mindlessness?"*

"You're the only one around, so you'll have to do."

"Thanks."

"You're welcome. Now let loose with the ideas."

"All right. How about if we—"

"Wait a second."

A gangly, sloppy-dressed teen boy passed them, heading straight for a short elderly woman who had just left the Corner Newsstand. He was moving quickly but quietly, his scuffed white tennies barely making a sound on the concrete. His left arm was held out, his hand open and directly in line with the woman's oversized black purse.

Rand thought

(*have a nice trip*)

and the teen stumbled, falling flat on his face. His head slowly came up. Looking like he'd just awakened from a deep sleep, he jerked his face around as if he had no idea what happened or where he was.

Oblivious to him, the woman reached the end of the block and crossed the street.

Harriet held back a laugh. *"Not bad."*

"Thanks."

"One thing, though. For future reference?"

"I'm listening."

"Please try not to hurt anyone, all right? We don't hurt mortals."

"But it was so much fun. And the kid was an asshole."

"I agree. Even so..."

He nodded. *"I gotcha. Let's go find Nadine."*

Harriet moved her robe-clad arm in a swirl of white.

A cluster of smoky clouds appeared, swallowing them both.

CHAPTER 14

His nerves finally under control, Monty leaned back in the leather seat and blotted his forehead delicately with his monogrammed hankie.

Thirty feet to his left, the motel lobby blazed with its floodlights. Nadine snoozed quietly beside him, her head tilted, her hair covering her left shoulder and part of the seat harness.

The dash clock said it was almost seven.

What the hell am I doing here?

Why hadn't he dropped off Nadine?

For some reason, I drove out of town, got on the Interstate, and hightailed it here, *of all places…*

That idiot outside the Café had rattled his nerves. Monty hadn't realized what he was doing or where he was until he got off the Interstate.

But he *had* planned on coming out here later on.

Damn. It's been a long time since I've been that angry. I've got to chill, or my blood pressure will soar again.

He needed a drink. Badly.

Nadine probably wouldn't even stir for a while. It was a shame he couldn't enjoy a full meal while he was here. There just wasn't time.

But he *did* have time for one drink. Just to settle his nerves.

He slipped quietly out of the Caddie and eased the door shut.

***

Her head warm, Nadine opened her eyes.

Floodlights. A building.

Trees. Bushes. Parked cars.

A *parking lot*?

Instantly awake, she sat up sharply.

Straight ahead, the well-lit brick building practically glowed in the dark. To her right, streetlights pierced the blackness of the night. Behind her, more trees and trimmed bushes decorated the grounds. A neon sign farther down lit up the sloping hill. Floods splashed a soft haze at the building.

Looked like the La-Z Inn off Interstate 70.

How did she get *here*?

Last thing she remembered was the Barnes Café—

Monty and the waiter fussing over her, helping her

("*you shouldn't drive home*")

into the Caddie.

Her pulse fluttering, she explored her surroundings. Leather seats. Shiny wooden dash. Padded console. Silly blue foam dice dangling from the rearview mirror. The lingering smell of Monty's French cologne.

This was Monty's Caddie, all right.

But where's Monty?

Her head grew hotter. *Oh my God.*

Niemus hadn't taken her home, he'd brought her here. All that stuff about helping her keep her house…seeing that she'd be taken care of…

This was how he intended to take care of her.

104

She fumbled for the catch of the harness, her hands shaking as they slid down the strap in the dark, not finding anything, groping—

She managed to free herself. Now, get the door open.

Once again she was all thumbs, probing, rubbing, exploring, trying not to panic. She found the lever and pulled. She must have had most of her weight pressed against the door; when it opened, she nearly spilled onto the pavement.

He was probably in the lobby right now, buying a room. She didn't want to meet up with him, didn't want to be anywhere *near* him. Her only option was to reach the walkway crossing over the Interstate, call a cab, and maybe have a cup of black coffee and a couple of aspirin at the truck stop.

Her heart sputtered wildly, but her mind was clear. A quick scan of the main entrance dictated her escape route. Still no Monty, but he'd be coming down the walk any time now.

If she circled around through the back, she wouldn't meet up with him.

***

Mindful of the sleeping shape beside him, Ralph Connelly groped for his clothes in the dark.

The night was going well. While Rachel dozed, he'd get more ice. When he came back he'd nudge her awake and they'd have another drink. He almost had her convinced to phone the other buyer in the morning and tell him that the country club estate was sold. Just a little more coaxing and the deal would be in the bag.

He slipped on his trousers and shrugged into his shirt. Then, ice bucket in hand, he snuck outside. His bare feet slapping the cool concrete, he hurried down the walk.

He was halfway to the ice machines when the familiar voice tore through him.

"Connelly? What the hell are *you* doing here?"

He spun around. Monty Niemus was standing in the breezeway, halfway between the lobby and the entrance to the Shamrock Lounge.

"Mr. *Niemus*?"

"Good guess." The man's broad cheeks splashed red in the motel lighting. His narrowed eyes were on Ralph's ice bucket as he came closer. "Tell me you're not shacking up here tonight."

No reason Niemus should know his personal business. But now wasn't the time to tell the arrogant jerk where to stick it. Ralph needed to get back to the motel room. Rachel might decide to take off if she woke up and found herself alone in a strange place.

Ralph kept his voice down. "I know how this looks, but—"

"Don't pull that innocent shit on me. I've been where you are too many times before." He risked a quick glance behind him. "You need to get the hell out of here before—"

"Listen…I've got this hot deal in the works, and—"

"I can imagine. How hot *is* she?"

Ralph's cheeks buzzed. Niemus had no room to talk. He'd often bragged about being the biggest stud in the county, how he could get any woman just by reaching into his pocket and peeling off a couple of fifties. "It's not what you're thinking—"

"*Ralph?*"

Startled by the sound of her voice, he whirled around. Nadine was standing at the end of the walk. Even in the hazy light of the breezeway he could see the astonishment on her face.

"*Nadie?*" Gripping the ice bucket in both hands, he hardly felt the cool concrete beneath his feet as he trudged past Niemus. "This isn't—"

She'd already turned on her heel and darted away.

Behind him, Niemus said, "Connelly, you're an idiot."

He wanted to belt the man. But it wouldn't be the brightest thing to do. Monty had too many connections.

Besides, he was about to make Ralph rich.

This would have to be handled delicately. Nadie had let him off the hook before, but this was way over the edge. A woman could forgive you much easier if she only *suspected* you were messing around. When she caught you at a motel half-dressed, carrying an ice bucket, it was a different ballgame entirely.

He'd have to be his most charming, convincing self. He'd been a salesman all his life—no reason he couldn't sell a little innocence and misunderstanding to a woman who was supposed to love him for better or for worse. Everything would

107

be fine. He couldn't piss away the deal of the century because of some stupid misunderstanding.

He bolted to the end of the walkway. Nadie had already crossed the main road.

CHAPTER 15

The heavy Wheeling-bound traffic roared beneath her as she reached the overpass. Trembling beams of headlights zoomed past.

Out of breath and shaking, the hot tears blurring her vision, Nadine snatched the cell from her purse. *I hate you, Ralph Connelly…*

The air was cool, the traffic deafening. Foul river air swooping up the valley mixed with the swollen clouds of exhaust fumes.

One false move would put an end to *all* her problems.

It wouldn't be so bad, would it? Stumbling on the concrete? Toppling over the side? Rolling down the hill and ending the torment in just a few painful seconds?

But it wouldn't be a *sure* thing. She could end up in an ICU ward, broken and shattered, receiving nourishment and medication from tubes and needles for the rest of her days.

Life was filled with enough uncertainties. Ending your existence had to be something definite…something well-planned and carefully thought out.

Something you couldn't mess up.

She pulled her cell out of her purse and pressed *talk*. A faint bleep. Stupid things *never* worked. She couldn't remember the last time she'd recharged it.

She'd have to hoof it across the walkway and use one of the payphones at the truck stop.

Ralph, how could you put me through this?

Ignoring her stinging cheeks and neck, she shoved the cell back into her purse. She wanted to toss it, to get rid of at least *one* thing that irritated her tonight. And since running back up the slope and gouging out Ralph's eyes wouldn't be practical, she might as well just toss the stupid thing.

But it would be silly, and she'd have to buy another one in its place.

She caught herself staring once again at the jittery trail of lights zipping beneath her.

Yes, that would be too easy. Knowing how life worked, she could see Monty paying off her mortgage and buying the house from Ralph. Ralph and "Miss Hayworth," no doubt the woman he was entertaining at the motel, would trot off happily into the sunset with their earnings. Nadine would be the ultimate loser.

Dead at thirty, the victim of three selfish opportunists.

And just what had she done in those thirty short years?

She'd been good student in high school, fairly popular with her classmates. She'd completed a year in a pre-med program, earning good grades and showing considerable promise before her parents' deaths forced her to postpone her education to take care of the estate. A couple of years as a doctor's assistant, showing great potential until the doc died, forcing her out of the career she loved and into a job she didn't want so she could afford to stay in the house she'd bought the year before.

Ralph entered her life, complicating things even more. Ralph and his dreams. Constantly wandering off to "amass his fortune," staying away for months, failing, then begging forgiveness.

But since Ralph had just proven where his interests really were, what did she have to look forward to?

Facing the rest of her life alone?

Her illness cutting it short by forty years?

Before she realized what she was doing, her leg came up and moved over the wall, straddling it, the cold concrete pressing against her calf. She swayed a little, the violent column of chilly wind shifting her balance while swatting her in the face.

What are you doing? a soft voice inside her asked.

I wish I knew.

You've never done anything this stupid before. Maybe the desire has always been there.

What desire?

Wanting to end things quickly.

You must be joking. Now pull your leg back and stop this nonsense...

A strange male voice behind her made her stiffen.

It was undoubtedly Ralph. Or Monty. They were probably looking for her so they could coax her back to the motel.

When she turned, she saw right off that it wasn't Ralph or Monty. It was that guy she'd bumped into just as she was entering the Barnes

Café. The man with the soft brown eyes and the nice smell…

She squinted. The orange strands of light spiraling down the nearby streetlamp distorted his features, changing his appearance drastically.

It was someone she hadn't seen in years. Someone she hadn't expected to see ever again.

No. It couldn't be. She was hallucinating. Of course she was.

Because in that same instant she imagined herself back on Main Street, fifteen years old again, one second away from being hit by the sportscar whipping around the corner.

In her state of dark depression, she'd conjured up all sorts of crazy images. This had to be one of them.

Rand Powell was standing behind her, inches away, reaching out.

"Rand?" His name tore hotly out of her throat. Its mere utterance brought about waves of dizziness. She hadn't said his name aloud in fifteen years.

He blinked. Something glittered in his eyes.

Her heart quivering, she watched her arms reaching out for him.   Dizziness beckoned, destroying her equilibrium.

Her footing gave way, and she stumbled. Then she fell.

CHAPTER 16

The shock waves rippled through Rand, turning the blood in his borrowed body into chunks of ice.

Oh my God...

What the hell *happened?*

Was this some sort of supernatural computer glitch? Did things actually screw up in the afterlife?

Forget about that—at least for the moment. Save the questions for later, when she's away from that damned rail and you don't have all that roaring tonnage raging beneath you.

Rand reached out for her. She'd already gone limp, her eyes closed, her head resting in the crook of his elbow, her hair jerking wildly in the wind. Her weight forced him off balance, and they both went over the rail. A bright flash of cascading light erupted around them.

An explosion of warmth encircled them. Rand hadn't noticed himself drifting downward, hadn't even felt the tire-hot pavement rushing up to warm the bottoms of his tennis shoes...but there he was, standing in the middle of the Interstate, her limp form in his arms.

Another flash of light. The traffic had stopped.

"So what do you plan on doing next?" Perched on the edge of the bridge, her robe wavy swirls of white, Harriet looked down at them.

"Next?"

"As opposed to now."

"I'm still trying to figure out what just happened."

"I've already told you, silly. Things are different for us."

Cars cluttered four lanes of highway, not one of them moving. Even the sounds of their idling engines had decrescendoed into an almost inaudible hum.

"This is really cool."

"I'm glad you approve. But you can't just stand there like that."

He barely heard her. The only thing that mattered was the woman in his arms. This was the same young girl he'd thought about and dreamed about for years. He'd finally come back for her. She didn't weigh much at all. Holding her made him feel more alive. He could stand here forever like this.

"You heard me, didn't you?" Harriet's voice jarred him back.

"I heard you."

"At least you're paying attention…"

"What's the rush? Are the guys upstairs in a hurry to get the traffic situation back to normal?"

"She's bound to wake up any time now," she said, an edge to her voice.

He hadn't thought of that. But it certainly destroyed the magic of the situation. He regarded Nadine's beautiful sleeping face and didn't want to do anything to interrupt her slumber. When he'd told Harriet he could stand here forever, he'd meant it.

"*Now* what's the problem?"

"Problem?"

"You're not moving. And you look even more confused than normal."

"Confused? Me?"

"Tell me the problem…" A reddish glow emanated above her head.

He studied Nadine's sleeping profile. "I'm enjoying myself."

"You're not serious."

"She feels…really nice."

"You're serious, aren't you?"

"It's been fifteen years."

"We have work to do. We're here for a specific purpose—which *doesn't* include your standing there in the middle of the Interstate."

"Are you sure my body's just borrowed?"

"Why?"

"I'm…getting excited."

"You're *such* a mess. Take her back."

"Back?"

"The motel—where else?"

"From here?"

"Will you *please* stop the nonsense and bring that girl up here?"

The hill leading up to the path, a 45-degree angle of grass, weeds, and dirt ascending forty or fifty feet, offered nothing to grab onto. And carrying an unconscious woman wouldn't make it easier.

"That's quite a climb."

"Need I remind you," Harriet said tiredly, "that you managed to get *down* with no problem?"

"I'm still wondering how I swung that one."

"Don't bother. It happened, all right? That's all you need to know."

"I'm distracted."

"Focus, Romeo. And start remembering. It just might come in handy later on."

He slipped between the motionless cars. The drivers sat still, in shadow. Ghosts. Shapes. Three-dimensional photographs.

Scaling the hill required no effort; Nadine was no heavier than down. When Rand reached the walkway, a roar erupted behind him.

The traffic was moving again, as if it had never stopped.

A tall, skinny guy around thirty was standing just a few yards from the walkway, his mouth open, his eyes tightly shut. An empty ice bucket sat in the grass at his feet. His hands covered his ears. His shirt was open, the breeze from the valley making his shirttails flutter like a flag, exposing his hairless belly. He remained motionless as Rand walked past.

Farther up the hill, his back to the Interstate, Monty Niemus hunched over. His eyes were closed, his face contorted into a frown.

A lanky black man in casual clothes and a Cincinnati Reds baseball cap waited in front of his cab near the motel entrance. As they drew closer, he opened the rear door.

Rand hesitated.

"Get in," Harriet whispered behind him.

He did as she said.

116

The driver closed the door and slid in behind the wheel.

"Lady all right?" He squinted in the rearview.

"She's had a rough day."

"Where'd you two come from? Didn't see you come outa the motel."

"Just down the road. Had a breakdown."

They eased away from the curb.

Rand sat back. Nadine hadn't changed much over the years. She still had the same little-girl quality he remembered so well. Her hair was just as full. It fell softly over his forearm like a warm curtain of golden silk.

"She recognized you." Harriet appeared beside him on the seat. *"She saw through your covering."*

"How did that happen?"

"Any ideas?"

"It might've been the eye thing that gave me away," he said after some thought.

"What eye thing?"

"It was like a scene in the movie, Here Comes Mister Jordan. *Near the end of the movie, Robert Montgomery tells Evelyn Keyes that one day she'll meet a guy with the same eyes—"*

"You've really got to stop this movie trivia stuff."

"--And that she should give the guy a chance. This was just before she meets the boxer she's supposed to fall in love with. Robert Montgomery was a boxer in the beginning of the movie, but he died when—"

"What's all that have to do with this?"

"I told you. This covering I'm wearing. She might have seen my own eyes."

"Impossible."

"What do you think happened?"

"Maybe she saw you because...because you were the one person she wanted to see at that particular moment."

"You really think so?"

"It's the only thing that makes sense right now..."

"I just hope she doesn't do that again. I won't be able to handle it if she sees my real face a second time."

"I don't think she will."

"But you're not sure."

"Right now, we can't be sure of anything."

"Hopeless," he muttered.

"Whazzat?" the cabby asked.

Rand sighed. "Just thinking out loud."

The cabby snickered. "I do that, too. You drive a cab, you do a lotta crazy things."

CHAPTER 17

Ralph sucked in a giant gulp of cool night air, ran the rest of the way down the slope and peered over the bridge.

Nothing.

How many drinks had he had? Three? More like six—maybe more.

But my mind is clear. Hell, a sight like that would clear anyone's head.

"Where'd she go?" Monty Niemus came up behind him and stared down at the loud roar beneath them.

"She disappeared." Ralph couldn't think of any other explanation.

"That's impossible." Niemus crossed the walkway and had a look at the other side, where the road led to the truck stop less than a mile away. "No one just disappears."

"Where'd she go, then?"

Niemus continued staring at the walkway. "There was someone else here. Some guy. Didn't you see him?"

Ralph *had* seen a shadow come up behind her, but everything after that was sketchy at best. He had the strangest feeling things had slowed down—although he knew that was impossible. "It was pretty dark."

"You mean to say you didn't see someone walk up behind her and pick her up?"

"Like I said, I'm not sure. I was too far away."

"How much have you had to drink?" Niemus asked.

"Not enough where I'm *seeing* things. How about you?"

"I've never been *that* drunk."

"Well, one thing's for certain." The chilly air made him shiver. He buttoned up his shirt. "If some guy did take her somewhere, he's got some explaining to do."

"I wouldn't jump the gun if I were you," Niemus said. "Whoever we're talking about might have saved Nadine's life."

Something occurred to him. "How'd she get here in the first place?"

Niemus sighed. "I brought her."

"I figured that. But why?"

Niemus suddenly looked guilty. "I needed a drink, all right?"

That didn't make sense. "And this was the closest place even though the Barnes Café serves drinks?"

"We had a nice long talk there about an hour ago, as a matter of fact."

"Who?"

"Your wife and me. Guess what the topic was. Let me give you a hint. It was about that offer you ran by me this afternoon."

God... If Niemus told Nadie about the mortgage deal, there would no longer be anything to work with. Niemus probably offered Nadie some sort of arrangement that would cancel out anything

Ralph wanted to do. The plan for the flip was history.

"Why did you decide to discuss that with my wife?" It was difficult keeping calm. "I thought we had a deal."

"I don't like people offering to sell me something they don't own."

"So you decided to discuss this with Nadie?"

"Connelly, there's one important thing you have to learn if you want to succeed in business. You need to play the hand you're dealt. Otherwise, you end up losing everything."

Monty Niemus was a lot of things, but honesty wasn't one of his qualities. Everyone knew that. And if Monty thought Ralph was unaware of it, he had another think coming. "Are you saying you told Nadie everything you and I—"

"All I said was that I'd help her keep the house."

"But...why would you do something like that when I told you—"

"It isn't your house."

"I'm her husband."

"Your name isn't on the deed."

"But—"

"When your name isn't on the deed, you don't have anything to work with. In other words, you fold your hand. It doesn't matter that you're her husband. It's her house."

"I still don't understand why—"

"Connelly, what's the best way of getting someone on your side?"

He didn't reply; he suspected Niemus was about to lecture him.

"The best way of getting someone on your side is to gain their trust."

Ralph tried to interpret what the man was saying, but with Monty you never knew. He spoke his own language when it came to business.

"So...did you succeed?"

"I wasn't able to get that far."

"What happened?"

"It seems that your wife is not much of a drinker. She passed out before I could tell her what was on my mind."

Ralph could only smile.

"This isn't amusing," Niemus snapped. "I plan on acquiring that house."

"I'm sure you are." An idea was already flashing in the back of his head. "I'd still like to be the one to help you acquire it."

"How? I don't think the woman will want to deal with either of us after what just happened. Your blunder—"

"My blunder might have actually *helped* the situation."

"How?"

"I'm now the bad guy."

"I'm sure right now she thinks both of us are."

"But you're the one who can save her by helping her with the mortgage, right?"

"That was my intent all along."

"Then do it. Otherwise, she'll lose the house. The bank takes it over and we're both sunk. Then you'll have to fight with other investors to get it. But if you can pick it up before the foreclosure, we're both still in the running."

Niemus was stroking his chin. "The problem I'm facing is that she thinks I brought her out here to get a room."

"By the way, how *did* you get her out here? Didn't she object?"

"She was out cold."

"She got in your car and just passed out?"

"I told her I was taking her home. *Then* she passed out."

This wasn't adding up. Niemus was obviously leaving something out. "But why did you end up out here?"

Niemus shrugged. "I wish I knew. Some bum gave me trouble when I was trying to pull out of my parking spot. He made me lose it, I guess. I just wasn't thinking clearly."

It still didn't make sense, but that no longer concerned Ralph. He was thinking of something that might work in their favor. When a situation messed up, you worked with it until you made it right. Niemus didn't think Ralph knew anything, but he couldn't be more wrong. And Ralph was just the guy to show him. "This could be our ace in the hole."

"How do you figure?"

"You could have come out here to talk to me. I called you on your cell."

"Why'd you do *that*?"

"To tell you I have a good chance of acquiring a choice piece of real estate."

"Why not just tell me over the phone?"

"I wanted to present it to you with the realtor present."

"Is that the chick you're shacked up with?"

"Yeah. What do you think of my idea? People conduct business at all hours nowadays. This wouldn't be that much out of the ordinary."

"I don't know. Your wife isn't stupid."

"No, but she's my wife. I can convince her of anything."

"Why would I want to know about your real estate deal?"

"Backing—why else? Nadie knows I don't have the money to swing any of this. If she thinks I'm trying to get you involved, she might also think I won't try anything with her house. She knows I've borrowed money from you before, so this'll be no different. She'll feel safe. And since her guard will be down, that's when you'll be able to move in."

"You're cold, Connelly."

"I like to think I'm highly motivated."

"But letting someone steal your wife's *house*?"

"You want it, don't you?"

"I need it."

"Then you work your side of the fence and I'll work mine."

"And you're sure there's no way for her to come up with the money?"

"The only thing she's got is a small savings account she's been adding to the last few years. It

124

might enable her to postpone a foreclosure. For maybe a month, anyway."

"Whose name is it in?"

"Ours."

Niemus' eyes grew. "Interesting."

"Now you've got the idea."

"So…what's next on your agenda?"

"A trip to town early tomorrow morning."

"Any special place?"

"The jewelry store. I need to buy something expensive," Ralph said, giving Monty his biggest and brightest grin.

CHAPTER 18

The taxi stopped in front of a cute two-story white frame house with green shutters and shrubbery showing definite signs of fall. A tall buckeye tree dwarfed the small front yard.

The cabby got out and held open the passenger door. With Nadine still in his arms, Rand carefully slid out of the seat.

The cabby slammed the door shut. "Well, g'night. Hope the little lady feels better." He tipped his cap, got behind the wheel and drove away.

Rand numbly watched as the taillights faded away in the darkness. Weird. Very, very weird.

"What's the problem now?" Harriet asked.

"He didn't...want money..."

"That's a good thing, isn't it?"

"It doesn't make sense."

"If he had *asked, would you have been able to give him any?"*

"Any change would've fallen through the holes in the pockets of my ensemble."

"Would you please *quit with the clothing editorial? We need to get her inside."*

He followed Harriet up the front stoop. The door yawned open.

"Hurry. She'll be waking up soon."

He stepped through the threshold, stopped, and stared. *"How the hell—"*

"Inside. No time to waste."

He followed her into a large, tastefully decorated living room. He laid Nadine down gently on a fluffy hunter-green couch and made sure her head was positioned properly on the pillow. When he turned, the door was closed.

"Did you *do that?"*

Harriet was standing behind the couch. *"Do what?"*

"Close the door."

"I'm over here with you. My arms aren't long enough."

"How did it close?"

"You didn't close it?"

She was playing games again.

"I had my hands full of unconscious woman," he said. *"A guy in my position isn't able to do much else."*

Harriet shrugged.

"You honestly don't know?"

"Don't know what?"

"Anyone ever say that you make a very poor dumb blonde?"

"I've also been told my Claude Rains is pretty bad, too."

Damn. Why did women have to have such good memories?

"So why didn't the cabby want money?"

"Maybe he forgot."

"A cab driver who forgets a forty-dollar fare?"

"Stranger things have happened."

"Uh-huh. Like that door closing on its own."

"It also opened on its own, didn't it?"

127

This was beyond strange.

"I guess I need to stop asking questions."

"I've been answering your questions."

"You call those answers?"

"Everything's no longer black or white where we are. Like I said, you'll get used to this. Just let it all happen."

Nadine moaned softly, shifting her head on the pillow.

"We're not finished with her," Harriet said.

"I just saved her life."

"This time, maybe..."

Her grim expression told him the worst. *"You mean there will be others?"*

"Most likely."

"This baffles me."

"Why?"

"How could someone with so much going for her have such lousy luck?"

"Life is full of mysteries. Everyone has problems, but not everyone can deal with them without help."

"It's not fair."

"Neither was being killed by a drunk driver on your way home, was it?"

"Well, it wasn't exactly the highlight of my afternoon."

CHAPTER 19

Her dream was a doozy.

It started off with her sitting in Monty Niemus' Cadillac outside the La-Z motel, fighting with the seat belt. Once she managed to get away she stumbled on Ralph, who was partially dressed, hiding behind an ice bucket.

This didn't make sense. Monty didn't care for Ralph because Ralph owed him money—so what were they doing at the motel together?

One thing *did* make sense: she knew what Ralph was doing there. And when the realization slapped her in the face, she turned around and ran.

And kept running. Running and running.

You were always a good runner. Since you were skinny, you could fly with nonstop energy. You could outrun the best of them, boys and girls alike. No challenge, really. A couple of quick strides and you were in the next county.

Tearing down the street, your long, braided ponytail thumping your back. Taking giant leaps, avoiding the cracks in the sidewalk. You had to avoid them because it was the way things were done. Proper, as Momma would say. Young ladies al- ways did things properly. Step on a crack, you break your mother's back.

Speaking of breaks . . .

Time for the first big one since lunch. Your favorite time of the day—when the last bell rings and the school buses come to the rescue. But you

*don't need to wait—your legs are faster and more
dependable than any bus.*

*Jogging home after school takes a lot out of a
girl—especially when your house is more than a
mile down the street. Next year you'll have wheels.
Cool. It was how the important guys got around.
Driver's Ed will be on your schedule. And what
goes hand-in-hand with Driver's Ed? Why, sister
Julie's classic Impala, of course. She promised to let
you learn in it, maybe even take it to a football
game. You could even drive around Dorothy and
Karen afterward and stop by the Pizza Palace in
Flushing, where everyone goes after a game.*

*Take it easy, now...you're at the Burger King.
Push open the glass door, plop down in one of the
curved white seats facing the street and wait for
Dorothy and Karen to join you. You always got here
first because they were* oh *so much slower. They're
bigger and don't have legs that come up to here.*

*Their chests slowed them down. When you're
hauling around a heavy rack, running can be
painful.*

So you were told.

*Not your fault your boobs hadn't yet made an
entrance. If you had your druthers, you'd look like
one of those Hollywood starlets. Next year, maybe?
Hopefully, because you're sick and tired of the way
everyone treats you. They stare constantly. You can
almost hear them saying,* where *are* they? *They
think there's something wrong with you. You're an
oddity.*

But you have other attributes. You've been told you're pretty. And everyone always says something nice about your cornflower blue eyes.

However, your favorite feature is that you move like a gazelle. You can use your speed to get away from whatever or whoever you want: bullies, stray dogs, passing traffic, school. Forget about your missing boobs: use those legs to get where you want to be.

Sitting alone and watching the traffic can be cool. You can think. Thinking is nice. You'll be a junior next year; you'll be expected to think more. Juniors are so much more sophisticated and smarter than sophomores because they're older, more mature, and spend their time thinking about college and their future. And since you got here first, you can watch the activity through the big front window and ponder the mysteries of life.

The Burger King's the only place in town where you can hang out with your buds. And it had great food. The juiciest cheeseburgers, the crispiest fries. Dilly Bars on a hot afternoon were the greatest things in the world. And even if you weren't hungry you could just hang around. Meg wouldn't care. Some grownups were okay. Not many, but some. Meg was amazing most of the time but talked about her arthritis too much, and it was so hard holding back hugantic yawns when she bragged about her daughters, who were married to successful lawyers. But most of the time Meg was pretty cool.

Dorothy and Karen had both already turned sixteen. Shame you just turned fifteen in January,

131

everyone constantly ragging you about it. The guys still treat you like a kid—pulling your ponytail, shoving you around.

But lately you've found out that life had somehow changed. For weeks you've been thinking about the strangest, most embarrassing things.

Not long ago you liked tree climbing, volleyball, running, and gymnastics. These were things you excelled in, that convinced everyone you were really cool.

But your interest in climbing trees fizzled out during the past year. And pinning a boy to the ground during recess—something you always loved doing—became a weird phenomenon of anxiety, confusion, and discomfort.

Dorothy and Karen said this would happen once you started having your period. Boy, were they right! They'd both started two years ago and knew what they were talking about. They told you what would happen, that it would change you totally. At first you thought they were kidding, but when you heard similar things from the other girls, you began to think differently.

You learned about sex several years earlier, but since it sounded weird, even funny, you hadn't paid much attention. But now, forbidden thoughts consume you. Instead of worrying about how well Barnes stacked up to the other teams in the area, you're mesmerized when your friends talk about their escapades with their boyfriends during the weekend.

132

Dorothy and Karen finally made it to the eatery, rushing breathlessly past and disappearing around the corner, where Meg stood behind the counter, getting ready for the rush hour crowd. A minute later Dorothy reappeared, licking the shiny white swirl topping her vanilla cone.

"Want one?"

"I'm okay." The chocolate shake at lunch had been enough. Besides, you're a little strapped at the moment and don't want to borrow any more money.

Dorothy stared at traffic for a moment, then went back to where Karen was, no doubt listening to Meg talking about her arthritis.

The beginnings of rush-hour traffic zipped past the window. In just a couple of years you'll be doing the same as everyone else: gulping breakfast, dashing off to work, rushing home after a long hard day, fixing supper, watching TV, and going to bed.

A downer. A big, fat downer.

Dorothy and Karen planned to get married right after college and raise a family, but you'd always had awesome dreams about moving to California to study medicine. Granddad and Grandma both died from lingering heart ailments. Watching them suffer was very traumatic. You'd wanted to help make them better. You even prayed that one morning they'd get up, healthy and young again and filled with vitality so they could dash outside with you and play badminton or toss some lawn darts. The fact that they'd gotten worse and worse, until they'd finally died, scared, and infuriated you.

All your life you've wanted to contribute, to lessen suffering. A career in medicine would satisfy that—

Her daydreams disintegrated in one baffling instant.

Whoa! Where did he come from?

The most amazing guy was standing on the other side of the street, waiting to cross. During a lull in traffic, he trotted across the two-lane road, heading straight for the Burger King and becoming more breathtaking with each step.

He was gorgeous. Curly dark-brown hair and the most incredible dark-brown eyes. Nice body, too. Wide shoulders, slim waist, and muscular arms. He was probably in his early twenties and was dangerously awesome in his red tee shirt. And those tight jeans made her dizzy.

Don't lose it. Be cool. A junior next year, remember? No need to stutter, blush, or do those other things nerds did.

But her body wasn't listening. Her cheeks had grown hot. Something large and warm had swelled in her throat and would have turned anything she said into gibberish. Good thing she wasn't expected to say anything. She would have died if Gorgeous had spoken to her. But he just slipped through the side door, smiled at her, and disappeared around the corner.

Everything stopped—the daydreams, the traffic, life itself. For the next few minutes, the only thing that existed was the image of the man's smile engraved permanently in her head.

It seemed like an eternity before the vision passed again, carrying two white bags. Her gaze automatically resumed its scan—that fine butt, the small waist, the shoulders, the dark-brown hair.

The glass door opened, and he no longer shared her space.

He jogged across the street, climbed the front steps of the house at the corner and disappeared inside.

CHAPTER 20

Nadine opened her eyes.

The darkness was oddly familiar.

Her living room, of course. She'd fallen asleep in her living room.

This didn't make sense because she didn't remember being in the room—not since this morning, anyway. What about the dream? It sure was weird. She was running away from Monty Niemus and Ralph, but she was fifteen again.

Nausea set in. The seat harness. The floodlights of the La-Z Inn. Monty and Ralph behind the motel. Monty in his expensive suit, Ralph half-dressed, an ice bucket in his hands. Her flight to the interstate—

Rand.

Had he finally come back? Or was he part of her dream?

She was exhausted and upset. The last few days had been horrible. It was only natural that she'd revert back to happier times. And since her childhood was the best time of all, she'd brought it all back and—

No...Rand was right behind her when she stumbled on the walkway.

But what was he doing there?

And why did he look like someone else at first?

It had to be a dream. Nothing else made sense. He'd been in the back of her mind for fifteen years, settled comfortably in the special resting place he'd fashioned for himself in her heart.

Enough. The exhaustion was doing strange things to her head.

Her limbs stiff and heavy, she got up. The room began to spin. She braced herself against the arm of the couch and waited for her equilibrium to return. When the motion gradually settled into a subtle distortion, she approached the staircase.

Holding on firmly to the banister, she decided to take it one step at a time. There was no need to rush. Rushing would be disastrous; she'd fall or throw up. Or both.

Exhaustion kicked in by the time she'd reached the top step. Luckily her bedroom was only a few feet down the hall.

Peeling off her clothes quickly turned into a major effort. They'd become tight in places, sweaty in others. The throbbing in her temples had already joined forces with the exhaustion, letting her know that the night ahead would not be pleasant.

No problem. She'd call the store tomorrow morning and tell Artie she was sick. She needed the time off, anyway.

This was Monty's fault. And Ralph's. And hers for having the wine in the first place. But mostly Ralph's.

Where was he? Still working on his "deal"?

Maybe he *was* at the motel. Maybe that *wasn't* a dream. The more she thought of it, the more she realized that she *hadn't* imagined waking up in Monty's car. The lush interior, the tacky foam dice, the smell of his cologne…was all *too* real.

If only the Rand issue could be explained…

Maybe she'd tripped in her attempt to get away from Monty and Ralph and passed out in the grass.

So how did she get home? Had Ralph brought her? If so, he'd be in the house.

But the silent darkness—and the absence of his strong Stetson scent—only made things more bewildering.

The wine would explain her confusion. Drinking— especially on an empty stomach— caused all sorts of illusions. She probably wasn't even near the Interstate in the first place. She'd already decided Rand was only part of the dream she had later. The overpass incident was probably part of it, too.

It was the only thing that made sense.

Catching Ralph at the motel with the ice bucket was very traumatic. Instead of confronting him there, where Monty and anyone else could listen to their private business, she decided to get as far away as possible. In her drunken clumsiness, she'd tripped and hit her head. Since her plan was to cross the Interstate and call for a cab, she'd dreamed that it actually happened. And since she was also thinking of the old days, when life was much kinder and simpler, memories of Rand came back.

That seemed to make sense.

But what *didn't* make sense was how she'd made it back home and had woken up on her living room couch.

***

From the dimly lit hall, Rand stared at the dark motionless form on the bed.

"Think she'll be okay?"

Harriet gave a deep sigh. *"For tonight."*

"What about tomorrow?"

"Tomorrow's another—" She tilted her head.

"What's wrong?"

"Someone's downstairs."

"Who is it?"

She blinked. *"I don't know. I'm up here with you, remember?"*

"Can't you, you know, use a little of that angel mumbo jumbo to feel who it is?"

"You can be so eloquent *at times,"* she said flatly.

"Let me guess. This isn't one of those times."

"And so bright."

"And you can be such *a woman."*

"Thank you for that glib but otherwise obvious comment." Then she disappeared.

CHAPTER 21

Nervous and exhausted by the evening's events, Ralph Connelly eased the kitchen door closed behind him, crossed the living room and tiptoed up the dark staircase.

His heart pounded as his brain flickered with frightening images of what he hoped hadn't actually happened. He kept telling himself Nadie had gotten home safely. He also kept telling himself that he hadn't seen what happened. The martinis had clouded his vision. Monty's, too—regardless of what the man said. Nadine couldn't possibly have fallen over the walkway and disappeared. They were much too far away, and it was dark.

What made much better sense was that Nadie had hitched a ride home with someone she'd met on her way to the truck stop.

That was what happened. She'd made it back safe and sound and was sleeping peacefully. All his worrying was for nothing.

But when you loved someone, you worried about them. He really did love Nadie—she was his wife. It wasn't his fault that he was forced to do something drastic with her house. He just didn't have much choice. It was the only thing standing in his way of achieving financial success. He didn't *want* to tap into her savings; that was something else he had no control over.

He'd make it up to her; he surely would.

She'd been hoarding that money since he'd known her. She wasn't about to hand it over to him—especially now, after catching him at the motel.

But if he wanted his dream to take shape, he had to make major changes. He'd lied to Monty; the account was in Nadie's name. But that was no problem; he could forge her signature. He'd done it before.

If there was another way of getting Rachel to hold that piece of property for him, he hadn't thought of it yet. But he didn't have much time left, and his list of options had all but vanished.

You come up with it by the day after tomorrow and you'll have the house, she'd told him as he left the motel room.

Which gave him one day.

When Nadie discovered she had no money to bargain with, she'd be furious. But after Ralph had made his money, he was confident he could get back in her good graces.

He paused in the bedroom doorway.

Nadie lay on her back in the bed, sleeping peacefully.

Sighing in relief, he tiptoed back out in the hall. Then he snuck down the stairs and went down the hall that led to their study, where Nadie kept her financial stuff. He switched on the desk light. The last he remembered, she kept her bank books in the top drawer.

Sure enough, everything was right there.

He opened the passbook. His eyes lit up. Nearly five grand. More than enough to stall the foreclosure for a few weeks and plenty to buy an expensive gift.

He ripped a check from the book. He didn't know how much he'd be spending in the morning, but at least he knew what the cap was. He carefully signed her name.

"Naughty, naughty…"

What the *hell*?

He whirled around.

The dimly lit room scoffed silently at him.

You're losing it, Ralphie boy. Hearing voices now?

You're just tired. Get some sleep. Tomorrow will be a better day.

He folded the check and stuck it in his wallet. Tomorrow morning he'd pay a visit to the Barnes Jewelers as soon as the place opened.

Right now, he needed sleep. He was still wrecked from what happened at the motel but joining Nadie in the double bed wouldn't be very bright. Besides, he needed to get an early start and didn't want to wake her.

He squirmed out of his jacket, tugged off his tie and lay down on the loveseat beneath the rear window.

When his thoughts finally stopped looping, he fell asleep.

THE SECOND DAY

CHAPTER 22

Olivia, her black, knitted maid's uniform loose as always over her short, square frame, was waiting for Monty at the foot of the stairs. "Will you be taking breakfast this morning, Mr. Niemus?" she asked in her usual deadpan, almost bored manner.

"Of course I want breakfast. And make it snappy. I'm famished."

"What would you like, sir?"

"What I eat *every* morning, dammit. Two eggs, bacon, sausage patties—"

She shook her head.

Here we go again, he thought. Once again the little bitch was trying to cause trouble. "Problem?"

"Mrs. Niemus prefers me not to cook the sausage patties. Too much fat and cholesterol. "

"Olivia, who are you talking to?"

"Beg pardon?"

"Do I look like Mrs. Niemus?"

Olivia frowned as she usually did when she knew he was about to give her "the talk."

"Mrs. Niemus has brown hair, right? She's also slimmer than I am, shorter, and wears a lot of makeup. Oh, and one other thing. Mrs. Niemus is a female."

Olivia kept frowning and looking away, at the portrait of Nancy and the kids hanging on the living room wall. Monty wanted to fire her right here and now but didn't want to have to deal with Nancy when she came home and found her little friend and ally gone.

"I just thought—"

"I don't care what you thought. I own this place. I pay the bills. And one of the bills I pay is your salary. Mrs. Niemus isn't here. She hasn't been here for two days. She won't be back until next week, and I intend to enjoy every damned moment of it. And if I want sausage patties for breakfast, I'm going to have sausage patties for breakfast. Understand?"

A heavy sigh. "Yes, sir…"

"Two eggs, bacon, sausage patties, hash browns, toast, and a stack of pancakes with maple syrup. By the way, I want three sausage patties. Make sure they're dark on the outside and juicy in the middle. I like mine oozing with fat and cholesterol. And hurry. Like I said, I'm starving."

Without a word, Olivia waddled off to the kitchen.

Resisting the urge to plant the heel of his patent-leather Florsheim in the center of her wide fleshy butt, Monty unlocked his study door, went inside, and slammed it shut. It was time for a little peace and quiet while he planned his day.

He shared the fifteen-room Victorian estate with Nancy and their two children, Monty Junior, 8, and Lindsay, 6. The mansion was situated on twenty sprawling acres on the outskirts of Barnes, complete with guest house, tennis court, riding stables and Olympic-size pool. The entire package had cost him pennies on the dollar, bought for back taxes twelve years earlier.

The past few days were wonderful. With Nancy and the kids visiting her folks in Columbus, Monty was a carefree bachelor again. The house was peaceful and quiet. For the first time in years, he didn't have to explain his every move.

But he knew his freedom would come to a screeching halt much too soon. Once Nancy and the kids returned, his solitude would become a treasured memory.

Their marriage had started out fine, but gradually deteriorated into a state of mutual contempt. Monty's constant demands for privacy and the secretive methods in which he conducted his business dealings grated on Nancy's last nerve, forcing her to re-evaluate their relationship. Nancy was a demanding woman who required a lot of money to support her lifestyle. Monty's refusal to be totally open with her about his business affairs served as the catalyst for their communications problems.

Their last argument dealt with the Elm Street Project. She'd heard from her snooty friends that Monty was about to make a killing with a huge condominium deal, and badgered him relentlessly, demanding a partner- ship. But when he refused to talk about it, she flew into a rage, packed her bags and the kids in her Town Car and left for a few days to stay with her family.

He suspected that while in Columbus, she'd seek out top-notch legal advice from her parents' family attorney and try a different tactic before coming home.

Monty had already talked to Sam, his personal attorney, and was ready for anything she might throw at him. The prenuptial Nancy had signed before their wedding had sealed her fate. There was no way she could get her paws on Elm Street or any of his other investments.

This morning, however, he faced a different problem. Oblivious to the sun peeking in through the French doors, he tried once again to make sense of what happened the night before.

He hadn't expected Nadine to collapse after a glass of wine. But hindsight told him the signs— heavy eyelids, slumped shoulders, garbled speech— couldn't have been clearer. He should have realized something wasn't right.

It was urgent to find out if she was all right. People had seen her with him, would suspect him if something happened. He had to somehow make everything right. He had no idea what he'd tell her when he did see her again but knew he could come up with something. He was a businessman; baffling people and distracting them were his stock in trade.

Connelly was an idiot if he thought their scheme could go on as though nothing happened. Connelly only proved his naiveté in the matter if he thought the previous night wouldn't change anything. Nadine had woken up at a motel when she'd expected to wake up in her own home. She'd caught her husband at the motel, gripping an ice bucket. And the man who'd been so caring at the

Café—who'd told her he'd take her home because she was in no condition to drive herself—was the culprit.

He dialed Connelly's cell phone. Hopefully the woman had gotten home somehow, and Monty wouldn't have to worry about her lying dead in a ditch somewhere.

Connelly answered on the second ring. "Mr. Niemus?" His voice was a whisper.

"Everything all right?"

"Nadie made it home safe and sound."

Monty sighed in relief. "How?"

"I haven't been able to find out. She's still sleeping."

"I take it you didn't join her."

"I didn't want to wake her. I've got things to do this morning."

"What we were talking about at the motel?"

"Exactly."

"Get it done right. Everything's got to happen quickly. And quickly, in business, means *now*. Got it?"

"Got it."

"It also means that if *I* lose, *you* lose."

"Don't worry. All I need from you is to have those papers ready for her to sign."

Monty hated a loser like Connelly talking to him like that. It was bad enough that he was getting no respect from his wife's maid and had to repeat himself for a simple breakfast request. But the world was rampant with idiocy, and even prominent men like him often found themselves standing knee-deep in it.

"They'll be ready," he told Connelly.

"And I'm taking your word that once this is in place, you'll advance me the money I need."

"Forty thousand—just like we agreed on. Provided you sign *my* agreement, of course."

"Of course. But I'll need that forty thousand the moment she signs the papers."

Monty didn't like this jerk's tone. Connelly was about to screw his wife out of her house and was only worried Monty wouldn't do the right thing. "I said I would, Connelly. I say what I mean. You don't say what you mean in this business, word gets out *fast*."

"Just making sure we understand one another."

"Oh, we understand one another, all right." Monty hated having this clown in the middle of his big project, but it was unavoidable. Connelly just didn't have the experience—or the savvy—it took to get things going. In time he might. But Elm Street was not the right project to risk on an amateur. "What bothers me is that I won't know when she'll want to talk to me again. I want this sewn up by tomorrow, at the latest."

"Call her today—any time after one o'clock. By that time, she'll have found out what I did. If I know her, she'll be ready to sign anything you offer her."

Monty hung up. Maybe he'd underestimated the smooth-talking son of a bitch.

148

CHAPTER 23

Beyond the tall pines peppering the valley, clouds drifted across the cosmic ocean of sky.

Nadine's house appeared lonely and forlorn. Dried-up yellow leaves skittered across the front stoop with the sharp morning chill. The buckeye tree shivered in despair.

Rand waited at the corner down the street as the morning unfolded.

Only moments ago, when they'd left Nadine sleeping peacefully in her bed, it had been night. By the time they'd left the kitchen and had gone down the back steps, the morning sun was already climbing the horizon. Harriet had said time was different for them, but it hadn't registered until now.

But as beautiful and as mystifying as all this was, it couldn't eclipse what was worrying him.

"Her life sure took a downward spiral," he told Harriet. "She's married to an idiot, is about to lose her home and has Niemus on her back. This is beginning to sound like a bad soap opera. Or one of those Country and Western love songs. By the way, what was her husband doing downstairs last night?"

"He took one of her checks before he went to bed."

"For what?"

"No idea, but he signed her name."

"He sounds just as unscrupulous as Niemus."

"I did tell you she was in trouble, didn't I?"

149

"I can't help feeling guilty about what's happening. If I hadn't moved away..."

"You did what you had to. She had to grow up and get on with her life."

"What I did was the best thing I could think of at the time."

"So how was it?"

"How was what?"

"The trip."

"To Florida?"

"It's what we're talking about, right?"

"I was miserable the entire time, hating every mile, constantly wanting to turn back and obsessed with what I'd left behind."

"What did you leave behind?"

He sighed. "A big chunk of my heart."

The shiny black BMW backed out of the gravel drive behind Nadine's house. It inched down the road to East Main, then pulled out and headed west, toward town.

"I wonder where he's going so early," Rand said.

No reply.

Harriet had vanished again.

***

Eyes closed, the washrag covering her forehead, Nadine lay on the couch and hoped the Tylenol would start working soon.

Earlier she heard Ralph leave the house, then from her bedroom window saw the BMW backing down the drive. He probably had appointments to make, people to borrow money from.

He'd obviously slept on the couch—which was a good idea, considering the circumstances.

She hated what happened last night. How could she have put herself in such a predicament?

The answer was simple. Monty had lured her there, and now she was paying the price.

If only he'd done the honorable thing and taken her home, things wouldn't be so grim. She wouldn't have seen Ralph at the motel. She would have gone straight to bed, maybe even gotten rid of this stupid headache.

But Monty *hadn't* taken her home; he'd committed the unforgivable. Just strapped her into his Cadillac and rushed off to the first motel.

What Ralph did was even worse. There was no way she was going to live with a man who was so preoccupied with making his fortune that he was with another woman when he should have been home, asking his wife about her test results.

That was what hurt most.

Not only did he want her to sell the house, but he also chose to share his bed with another woman while his wife, sick and depressed, seriously contemplated jumping from the overpass.

She sat up sharply. The washrag slid from her forehead. Ignoring the thumping in her head, she struggled to make sense of everything. But just when she thought she had it together, something else crawled in there

(I fell)

to upset the works.

She *had* fallen, hadn't she? It *couldn't* have been a dream. She heard a voice, spun around, lost her balance, and fell. At first she'd blotted it out, told herself it was an illusion.

But was it?

She'd reached out and groped for him. Even caught the edge of his hand with her pinkie. He *wasn't* a hallucination; he was *flesh and blood*.

It *was* Rand standing there, gaping at her just before she fell into the roaring chasm.

It wasn't possible, was it? There was no way she could have fallen without breaking something…or worse.

Maybe she only *thought* she'd fallen.

When you're confused, upset, and depressed, all sorts of pictures spin wildly in your head. It's only natural that your mind would tell you things that didn't make sense. Why shouldn't your subconscious turn your dilemma into a series of beautiful images? Why shouldn't it try to make the unpleasantness tolerable?

So while you only *thought* you'd fallen, you may have stumbled the other way, landing on the concrete floor of the walkway.

Someone driving to the motel or from the Mall spotted you and called it in. Lots of people tripped or stumbled on the overpass. You're engrossed in the loud violence of the traffic and the wind rushing up from the valley. You're distracted. You lose your equilibrium, then your footing. At night it would be even more disorienting.

The paramedics laid you down on a gurney, took your vitals and brought you in for tests. When they were satisfied you were okay, they released you.

That was the most reasonable explanation of all. The only thing that could've happened.

But none of this explained her most important question.

How did I get home?

CHAPTER 24

One block down the street from Nadine's house, three grade school kids were picking on a smaller kid at the bus stop, taking turns shoving him into one another. The victim was crying, trying to get away, but was quickly grabbed and yanked back into the circle of terror.

Rand remembered the times in his youth when he'd fallen victim to similar tactics. He also remembered wishing he could do something to stop his attackers.

He couldn't then, but now that things were different, he had just the remedy that would turn the tables.

He thought, *Banana peels*.

Gasping loudly as their feet were swept out from beneath them, the three aggressors rolled around on the pavement, then struggled to get back up, but slipped on their books and backpacks.

Their victim had fled.

"What are you up to now?" Harriet had reappeared behind him.

"Having a little fun in the morning sun."

"Didn't I tell you to stop hurting mortals? You'll never be one of us if—"

"I was reminded of my childhood."

"We're only supposed to act on something if it helps the situation."

"It sure did help the poor kid those little assholes were knocking around."

She shook her head. "Sometimes you're *so* tiring…"

"But entertaining, right?"

"I'm laughing every minute."

"Where were you, by the way? Shadowing Nadine's idiot husband?"

"He's definitely up to something nasty."

"Does this have anything to do with that check he took last night?"

"It very well might. He went into the jewelry store as soon as it opened."

"That doesn't make any sense."

She smiled. "Maybe he's buying her something to make up for last night."

"With *her* money?"

"You're right." Harriet's smile quickly vanished. "I guess I was hoping he wouldn't be as worthless as he appears."

"You're an angel. You have to see the best in mortals."

"Sometimes it's a real chore."

"With her husband and Niemus, I think it's downright impossible."

"Lighten up," she said. "Your attitude shouldn't be so cynical."

"That's going to take a lot of adjustment…"

"Don't worry about that yet. Let's just concentrate on our mission."

"All right. So what do we do next?"

"Wait and see what develops."

"How long?"

"Until her husband screws up again."

155

"That shouldn't take long."

"Going by what we've already seen, it shouldn't take long at all."

***

Nadine sat at the kitchen table, finishing her orange juice.

The Tylenol had helped a little. She hoped the vitamin C would help make her less nauseous.

She hated calling in sick, but there was no way she could function at the store, feeling this bad.

The previous night's events trickled back. Not the Niemus or the Ralph part—the Rand part. It was much more satisfying.

But it wasn't right, thinking about a man from your past when you were married to someone else.

She didn't care; it felt right. Her marriage was rocky, to say the least. The separations alone made their situation almost laughable.

She couldn't help feeling sorry for Ralph even though what he was doing hurt beyond words. She wanted to cry because she knew she didn't love him. She thought she did, but it had never been that pure, breathless, heart-pounding thing you read about in romance novels.

The thing with Rand happened when she was very young, but even though she was naïve and inexperienced, she knew it couldn't go on. She was fifteen and still a kid, although she felt like a grown woman.

She hated Rand for leaving, for deserting her. Hated him just as much as she loved him. What hurt her most of all was that she had given him so much of her heart. But he'd left anyway, taking part of her with him.

Why was she thinking of Rand so much lately?

That was obvious. Her life had been heading down the tubes for the last several years. Since her prayers hadn't been answered for so long, it was only natural to revert to happier times. And the happiest time of her life was the summer she fell in love with Rand Powell.

***

She must have stayed on that curved plastic seat in the Burger King at least an hour that strange afternoon, staring at the house her mystery man disappeared inside, her gaze darting from one shuttered window to the next, hoping for a glimpse of his shadow.

At one time she thought she saw him but realized it was only the glare of the sun winking at her.

Dorothy and Karen had finished their cones and wanted to hang out at the Five'n Dime for a little while, but Nadine stayed right where she was, telling them she just wanted to go home. When Dorothy asked if she was looking for that cute guy who'd just left, Nadine blurted out, "*What* cute guy?" And when Karen laughed and asked her why she'd been staring at the house where the cute guy had gone, Nadine could only turn away and stammer, "Mind your own business."

At supper she picked at her food while the birds chirped at one another from the sycamore outside the kitchen window. Momma and Dad made futile attempts at conversation, but she hardly heard them.

She went back out to the front porch later on and sat on the glider, watching the mystery man's house. When darkness came and there was still no sign of him, she went back inside.

She didn't see him for the longest time. It turned out to be only a week or so, but back then it seemed an eternity.

The next "sighting" occurred on a bright Saturday morning.

She'd just had breakfast with the family. Julie, her oldest sister, and Christa, Julie's college friend, had stopped by. Wanting to be by herself, Nadine went outside and sat down in a lounge chair in the back yard.

Only minutes later she saw him through the opening in the picket fence.

He was wearing cutoff jeans and tennis shoes and carrying pruning shears and a rake. He had a beautiful body—lean with noticeable muscle.

For more than two hours she watched him trimming the bushes along the side of the house at the corner. Her imagination ran wild. She visualized herself running over and helping him, handing him things, rubbing against him, running inside to get him something to drink.

She remained at his side until he finished, then followed him inside and helped him out of his damp, sweaty clothes before they stepped into the shower together—

***

The kitchen door yawned open.

Ralph poked his lean, guilt-ridden face through the opening. "Morning, babe."

She sat up. Daydreaming about Rand and then being interrupted by her pitiful husband sneaking into the house like a whipped puppy made her head pound even more. She tried turning Ralph into Rand, if only visually, but it just didn't work. It never did.

He closed the door and stood there awkwardly, not knowing what to do. He was holding something in his left hand. A black oblong jewelry case.

A peace offering?

Ralph didn't have the money to buy jewelry. He'd probably used one of his credit cards again.

But it didn't matter. She wasn't as angry with him as she should be. Maybe it was because she was fantasizing about another man and felt guilty about it. Or maybe she was just too worried about her own situation to work up a good mad.

The last—and worst—possibility was that she just didn't care anymore. When the romance is dead and the trust gone, the relationship is nothing more than a bitter memory.

"Feeling any better?"

She wanted to laugh. "Not really."

"Maybe this'll make it all worthwhile." He handed her the case.

"What's this?"

He shrugged. "Just my way of saying I'm sorry."

"Ralph—"

"It's that necklace you wanted a couple of years ago."

Sure enough, it was the same one she'd lusted over but knew she'd never be able to afford. The same white diamonds, the same finely-cut emerald stones.

"Why did you do this? You know we don't have the money. I thought your credit cards are maxed out."

"They are."

"Then how—"

His sheepish grin told her the worst. No. He didn't. He wouldn't.

"Ralph...where did you get the money for this?"

No reply.

"This necklace costs nearly four thousand dollars. Where did you get the money?"

"I figured you wouldn't mind. I—"

"You didn't." Ignoring the queasiness, the heat swelling in her head, she left the necklace and case on the table and stood. "Tell me you didn't do what I think you did. Tell me. *Please* tell me."

"Listen, Nadie. I feel really bad about what happened, so I—"

She stormed out of the kitchen and went down the hall, to the den. Her fingers barely worked; grabbing the drawer pull and yanking it took a number of tries. But as soon as it opened, she gawked at the sight.

Her checkbook wasn't piled neatly on top of the stack, where she always kept it. It was tossed

160

carelessly. She groped for it, nearly dropping it, and opened it.

Ralph did what she suspected. The very worst thing he could ever have done. He spent her savings on—

"I wanted to make it up to you." He leaned against the open door, his grin not nearly as overpowering. "I felt bad for last night and figured—"

"You...*forged* my *name*?" She could barely get the sentence out.

"I didn't think you'd mind when you saw *why* I did it—"

She closed her eyes so she wouldn't have to look at him. Her limbs trembled; the heat smothering her neck made her skin break out in irritating blotches. "Ralph, take the necklace back." She was surprised her voice still worked.

"But—"

"Take it back this instant and get my money back."

"I can't."

"Why not?"

His grin vanished. He swallowed; he knew he was in serious trouble. "I had it...inscribed."

"You *what*?" The words tore from her throat like shards of glass.

"I thought it would be special if I had your name inscribed on it. "

"I don't *believe* what you...what you just did." She rubbed her eyes. The dizziness had turned into a sensation of distant humming.

161

"I'm serious. I thought—"

"My grandparents opened that account for me when I was little." Her voice sounded bizarre, but at least it worked. "They put a hundred dollars in it but didn't tell me about it because they didn't want me to spend it on anything stupid." The humming increased. Hot tears filled her eyes. "I was going to use it to make an interest payment on this house. It would have been the only thing to keep me from being thrown out into the street. And you've ruined it, Ralph. You've *ruined* it."

"Nadie…this could be a blessing in disguise. We could make a fortune on this house. Monty wants it badly, and he won't quibble about price. We can use the money to buy another—"

"I don't want to *hear* it!" She dropped the checkbook in the drawer, slammed it shut, and stomped past him. The urge to strangle him was so overwhelming, she had to force herself to keep her arms crossed in front of her as she stormed down the hall.

She passed the kitchen table. The necklace was on the table, mocking her. She didn't want to look at it. It symbolized a violation. The death of their relationship.

"Nadie." He'd followed her but kept his distance by staying close to the doorway. "I was with the realtor all day yesterday—"

"And all *night*," she said, leaning against the counter.

He ignored her comment. "Anyway, she gave me twenty-four hours—"

"What else did she give you, Ralph?"

"Nadie…"

"Did you have fun?"

"I thought I told you…it was business."

"And it lasted *all night*?"

"I had too much to drink and decided to spend the night at the motel."

"Of course you were alone."

"What makes you think I wasn't?"

"I know you, Ralph."

"I don't like your tone."

Her laugh was weak as it trickled out of her throat. It lacked humor and sounded more like a cough. It was so typical of him to turn this around. He'd done it before. The situation was indeed laughable. Their life together was dead, she was dying, about to lose her home, and he was nitpicking. "Before you get upset, let me put it this way. I just don't care if you were with another woman. One woman or twenty women—it doesn't matter anymore."

He swallowed. "What do you mean by *that*?"

"It's very simple. I want a divorce."

His face paled instantly. "Listen, Nadie…just because you think I was with someone last night doesn't give you the right to—"

"Ralph, it's not just that. You don't care. You don't listen to me. You don't spend time with me. You've been away for years, pursuing your dream. Even when you come back, you're still away. You've never been here for me. And here is where I need you. Especially now."

"You're just upset—"

"Of course I'm upset. It's not working. It's run its course. It's over."

"I've got this deal right now. If I can manage it—"

It was time to tell him about her condition. "I'm—"

"I'm sure I can, too."

"Ralph, I've got something to—"

"If you'll just let me do this, I think I can—"

Dear God..." She sighed. It was no use. As usual, he just wasn't listening. Even if she'd managed to tell him she was dying, he wouldn't have heard it.

He watched her, studying her eyes, possibly trying to read her expression. Then he scratched the back of his neck. "Listen, Nadie. I know you think everything's bleak and all, but—"

"Everything *is* bleak, Ralph..."

"Everything will be all right, I promise. This deal I'm working on? Once it breaks open, we'll have enough money to—"

"Stop it."

He said nothing. Maybe he finally realized what she'd said. Maybe not. He was so obsessed with his dream that it wasn't possible for him to understand anything else. She'd just tried to tell him she was dying...but it didn't matter.

"Nadie, we've been together five years now, and—"

"We've been married five years, but we haven't been *together*. We're two strangers living in the same house, and I'm tired of it. You have your life and I have what's left of mine, but you're just not interested in anything going on with me."

"But—"

"Admit it, Ralph. You don't care about me. It's all right. I don't care about you, either."

"How can you *say* that?"

"It was very easy, actually. That makes it worse because it tells me that we really *do* need to split up."

"Nadie, you're upset. I can't blame you. But last night—it wasn't how it looked."

"What would *you* think if you saw *me* half-dressed at a motel, carrying an ice bucket?"

"I'm glad you brought that up. What were you doing there?"

"Monty brought me there while I was asleep."

His frown told her how lame that sounded. And she couldn't blame him; it did sound downright lame.

"I was at the Café with him. We met there so he could present his proposal that would let me keep this house."

"And you fell asleep while he was talking?"

"He gave me some wine and I couldn't handle it. He offered to drive me. We went out to his car, and I just sacked out."

"And ended up at the motel?"

"That's what happened."

"How come I don't believe you?"

"Believe what you want. Like I said, I don't care anymore."

165

"Nadie—"

"Ralph, I'm going for a walk." Her sudden craving for fresh air was as strong as if she'd been locked in a coffin. Ralph had managed to turn the house she loved into a confining, suffocating prison she needed to escape. "I don't know how long I'll be, but when I get back, I want you gone."

"You're throwing me out?"

"I'm asking you to leave."

"But Nadie—"

"I don't want that necklace here when I get back, either."

She opened the kitchen door and closed it quietly behind her.

CHAPTER 25

Ralph couldn't believe his ears. Nadie wanted him out of the house. And she sounded like she actually meant it.

This wasn't like her. Nadie had never been the type to go off like that.

It was some sort of sentimentality hang-up, no doubt. She'd always been close to her grandparents. Doing what he did to the savings account they'd started up in her name had obviously been too much. And coupled with her financial troubles, the stress had done her in.

His cell buzzed. The display registered Monty Niemus' number.

Oh boy. This isn't what I need right now.

"What's going on?" Niemus asked.

He sat down at the table and ran a hand briskly through his hair. The necklace winked at him, telling him he was an idiot. But it also told him that maybe what he did wasn't so wrong. He needed Nadie to sell the house, didn't he? Well, the necklace would certainly make this happen. Now all he had to do was talk her out of the divorce.

"Connelly? You there?"

"Nadine wants a divorce."

A pause. "She *what*?"

"We just had helluva row—"

"This have anything to do with her finding you at the motel?"

"That's only part of it."

167

"What else happened?"

"I bought her an expensive necklace. The idea backfired."

"You idiot. I hope you realize what you've just done. If Elm Street—"

"I don't care about your damned project." It exploded from his throat before he had the chance to think it through. But he couldn't help it; his brain was having a meltdown.

After about ten seconds, Niemus said, "Did you just say what I thought you said?"

Calm down. Niemus can really hurt you if you get on his bad side. The best thing you can do is apologize and listen to what he has to say. He can still bail you out, but you have to put your personal feelings aside and let things take their natural course.

"I'm really sorry, Mr. Niemus." *Damn*, that was hard. It took him back to sixth grade, when he was caught by Mr. Phillips for carving Sue Ann Garsky's initials on his desk. "I...don't know...what got into me. I wasn't prepared for...for how Nadie reacted."

Silence at the other end. He really hoped he sounded sincere enough...

Niemus finally said, "I understand."

"Do you?"

"We're talking about women, aren't we?"

Ralph wiped his brow with his shirt sleeve. That was close.

But he was certain Niemus knew about such matters. Monty had been married a few times himself. Everyone knew Nancy had taken over Monty's mansion as well as his credit cards.

"Nadie's been under a lot of stress," he told Niemus. "It's not like her to blow up like that."

"This is why we need to work this just right."

"How can I do anything when she wants me out of the house?"

"She threw you out?"

"She went for a walk. I have to be gone by the time she comes back."

Niemus gave a low whistle. "She's *really* ticked at you, isn't she?"

Ralph didn't like the man's glib tone but decided not to press the issue. "The necklace was the last straw. I had no idea her grandparents opened that account for her when she was little."

"So you really *are* the bad guy. That was our original plan, wasn't it?"

"At least I got *that* right..." But it only made him feel worse.

"I think it might be time for me to step in."

"I don't know. Nadie's pretty upset. She might not listen—"

"Do you know how much that Elm Street project is worth?"

"Probably several million, for starters."

"Nine figures, Connelly."

"*God*..." Nine figures... That meant more than—

"*Now* do you see why I have to stay on top of all this?"

CHAPTER 26

Ignoring the tears staining her cheeks, Nadine descended the slope behind her house, where the woods ended a few yards from the creek running along the foot of the hill.

The wind whispered softly through the pines. Birds flitted from one tree to the next. The sweet smell of the grass and the pungency of the moss growing on the rocks lining the creek—elements she was so familiar with—now seemed foreign. Cold. Unpleasant. *You're a stranger*, everything seemed to say. *You don't belong here. Get out.*

It now belonged to Monty. The whole area would soon be his to destroy—the trees cut down and hauled off, the slope overflowing with apartment dwellings, the gravel paths gouged and widened to make room for roads strong enough to accommodate the traffic from the hundreds of new residents flooding the area.

She felt like a traitor. She wanted the trees to know that she tried, but there was only so much she could do. With people, the only thing that mattered was money. Without money, you were nothing.

Ralph, how could you take the only money I had left in the world?

How could you stand there when I was trying so hard to tell you I was dying and think only of your stupid business deal?

She sat down on a small grassy knoll a few yards from the stream. The afternoon sun turned the surface of the clear water into shimmering diamonds. Tiny tadpoles darted among the rocks. Microscopic bubbles popped up and exploded in silence. She wondered if Monty would leave the stream alone—if he'd have the decency to keep at least some of this pastoral beauty the way it was.

But she knew better. Monty cared only about profits. If the stream was blocking progress, he'd simply pay someone to fill it in.

All because of me. And Ralph.

If only I could go back in time, when I was a little girl and things were simpler… Life was fun, full of mystery and wonder. Tragedy and sadness hadn't yet touched my sphere.

She checked her watch. Would Ralph be gone by now?

She had no idea how long she'd been out here. She only knew she didn't want to go back and find him there. His presence would only deepen her depression.

She'd give him another half-hour. Then she'd start back up the hill.

If ever she needed a miracle, it was right now.

Miracles happened, didn't they? Or was she still clinging to that silly childish notion that life would always be sunny and filled with joy?

She remembered reading something about children believing in magic, but when they became adults, they no longer believed. She'd often wondered about that. She'd also wondered why she still believed. Thirty years old and she still clung to the strange feeling that magic indeed existed.

171

But what else was there?

Without magic, without hope, you might as well sleepwalk through life and wait for darkness to come and take you away.

She put her head in her hands. One more good cry would do it. Then she could go back to the house. The prospect of returning to an empty house didn't appeal to her. However, finding Ralph still there would be even worse.

She suddenly felt someone behind her. She hadn't heard approaching footsteps and thought she was imagining things. When you're upset and jumpy, your faculties play tricks on you. Like making you think you're somewhere you're not...or imagining someone from your past was behind you, reaching out for you.

But when she saw the glimpse of a shadow out of the corner of her eye, she nearly came out of her skin. She scrambled to her feet, spun around, and found herself looking into the beautiful soft-brown eyes of a handsome, sloppy-dressed man.

"I didn't mean to startle you." His voice was soft and gentle, like his eyes.

"It's all right." Despite her initial shock, she felt a strange sense of calm. "How long have you...been standing there?"

"Not long. Walking among the trees relaxes me."

"I like doing that, too."

"Do you do it often?"

"Not often enough." The last time was about a year ago, during Ralph's last departure. It had helped immensely. It was only after she'd returned to the house that the depression had kicked back in.

"There's nothing like surrounding yourself with nature," the man said. "It's very humbling."

"Yes. It is." She remembered where she'd seen him before. He was the man she'd bumped into outside the Café. Her reaction then—warmth, a feeling of contentment—seemed the same as now. Then she wondered if this man had somehow been in her dream the night before. She realized what must have happened. She remembered him from the Café—it was only natural that he should already be in her mind.

"Why isn't it helping?" he asked.

"Pardon?"

"Your walk. It's not making your situation any better."

She realized then that his beautiful eyes weren't only for show. "You see a lot, don't you?"

"Your tears *say* a lot."

She turned to wipe them away. She didn't want anyone to know what was wrong. It was bad enough all this was happening. It would be even worse if everyone in town knew about it. "I'm sorry. I'm just depressed."

"Never apologize, Nadine. Not for being sad."

She perked up. "You...*know* me?"

He nodded. "You work at the Five'n Dime."

Of course. She should have known he'd say that. Everyone said the same thing. She even heard it when she went to St Clairsville to shop for clothes. She didn't know why it disappointed her

173

right now. She guessed it was because she was hoping for something magical. The way he'd come upon her so silently had her puzzled. "I…saw you yesterday, didn't I?"

"Outside the Café."

"And…when Monty put me in his car?"

"That was me, too."

He'd tapped on Monty's window, then circled the Cadillac. The image was sketchy, but she clearly remembered the concern on his face. "What were you doing? I could hear shouting."

He shrugged. "I didn't have a warm feeling about Niemus. He told me he was taking you home, but I was afraid he was going to take you somewhere else."

"He took me to a motel." She had no idea why she was telling a stranger this sordid business, but she felt comfortable in his presence. "When we were there, I saw my husband. He was with another woman. My life has been falling apart ever since."

"I wish I could help."

"That's nice of you, but it's my problem. I've got to solve it somehow. By myself."

"Is it possible?"

"No, but whatever happens, I've got to do it myself."

"Couldn't you use some help?"

"Of course I could…"

"Then why won't you—"

"People just don't care about one another anymore. At least, they don't care about me."

"I do…"

174

He seemed so sincere. She couldn't help thinking that he actually believed what he'd just said. "But…I don't even know you."

"Why should that matter? You still need help, don't you?"

How could anyone help her? She needed money to keep her house, and even if she did manage to find enough money for that, how could anyone help her with her medical problem?

"I just don't see how anyone can do anything for me," she said.

"One never knows, right?"

"Where do you live? I don't remember seeing you before…before yesterday."

"I'm just visiting."

"From where?"

"Orlando, Florida."

"What are you doing *here*?"

"I used to live here a long time ago."

She couldn't believe this. Was she hallucinating? "When?"

"Several years."

"How many?" she asked softly.

"Around fifteen. You were a little girl with a long, braided ponytail."

This was getting stranger by the second. "Did I…know you then?"

"You were too busy running around, climbing trees."

Her face grew warm. She hardly felt the cool wind whispering through the trees and drying her tears. "What's…your name?" she asked in a whisper.

"Jerry."

"What did you do…when you lived here?"

"I was renting apartments. Collecting rents for them. My family owned one on East Main. Just two doors down from where your folks lived. The century house at the corner, across the street from the Burger King."

My dear God. The house Rand lived in.

This man…this Jerry…owned the house. But wait a minute. Something didn't make sense. "I thought a man named Jack Sherwood owned it."

"Jack was my grandfather."

Nadine swallowed a warm, gooey lump. "Mr. Sherwood…was your *grandfather*?"

"Sure was."

"You have no idea how *weird* this is."

"Speaking of weird…I need to ask you a question," Jerry said.

"Yes?"

His soft brown eyes stayed on her when he said, "Do you believe in magic?"

The dizziness made the pines sway in strange directions. The wind changed, cooling her face, then her hands. The sun went down and a moment later it looked like night had swooped down upon her. The blackness clouded her vision.

Something caught her just as she felt herself falling to the ground.

***

Rand carried Nadine up the grassy slope.

176

"All right, Romeo," Harriet said, following him. "What's next?"

"I'll think of something." He was staring at the woman sleeping in his arms.

"This is nothing to trifle with, you know."

"Who says I'm trifling?"

"Your face. You're grinning like an idiot."

"How am I supposed to grin?"

"You could show way less teeth."

"I can't help it. Like I said before, she—"

"Feels really good. Yes. I remember."

Rand said nothing, but his grin relaxed—but only slightly. Carrying Nadine was doing him a world of good. He didn't even care that he was dead anymore.

"You're playing with a woman who has been going through severe depression."

He stopped walking. "I'm trying to help her the only way I know. You keep telling me this is my ballgame, that I'm the only one who can do this. Let me do it. Get with your cohorts up there calling the shots and tell them to give me some space. They wanted me in this, so they got me. And I have no intention of standing around like an idiot, asking you what I should do. In case you haven't noticed, I'm not a little kid and you're not my mother."

"Thank you for that obvious but somewhat callous comment…"

"You keep saying I'm a hard case. Well, maybe I am."

"No maybes about it."

"I am what I am—as Popeye would say."

"Will you please stop the trivia nonsense?"

"One day, maybe."

"But not now?"

"Too many other things on my mind at the moment."

"Like what you're going to do when you take her back inside?"

"That's pretty high on my list, yes." He carried her up the rear steps leading to the kitchen.

CHAPTER 27

Monty pulled up to the curb and killed the engine.

At the end of the walk, the shuttered windows of Nadine's house eyed him suspiciously.

You're just agitated from last night. And, of course, from Connelly's blunders. But bear in mind that what Connelly did will probably get you this house much easier.

It was going to be a sweet deal. Once the house was in his name, they'd be able to break ground early in the spring and finish within two years. Nadine's house and the other three fronting the block would be torn down to make room for the four-story brick buildings that would run the full block and nearly three-quarters of the way down the slope, where the land would be cleared to make way for the recreation center that would be put in for the new residents.

But this had to be done with utmost care. Without Nancy finding out.

"You have to handle these issues in order," Sam Wade, his lawyer, had told him only two days earlier, in Monty's South Street office. "You need to concentrate on getting your wife out of the picture with a solid divorce settlement first. Ohio, as you well know, is an equitable distribution state. That doesn't necessarily mean equal, but it does mean fair. And if Nancy finds out the particulars about Elm Street, she'll certainly get her high-powered family attorney to work on nullifying the prenuptial on the basis of deception on your part, work on getting as much as she possibly can from it, and make for one lousy bad time for both of us."

Monty knew Sam was right. But in such matters, Sam was always right.

"It'll be tricky," Sam said, "but I think you might be able to do it. Take advantage of the fact that Nancy's in Columbus. Anything you decide to give her other than what is spelled out will be a plus on your part. It'll make you look better, and the settlement might go quicker. Any other trump cards you have besides the fifty-five T-Bird she wants so badly?"

"I've got a good-looking chunk of dirt she's always wanted, but it's worth too much to just hand over."

"That property adjacent to the Interstate Mall?"

"Forty prime acres. I got it on the sly."

"Put it on the table."

"I dunno, Sam. Five years from now? That parcel will be worth well in the seven figures."

"The Elm Street project's worth ten times more. Once you get Nancy to agree to a satisfactory settlement, you're home free. Just remember this: losing a hundred-and-fifty-thousand-dollar pivotal property capable of generating between five and eight million a year will be much more disastrous than any divorce settlement."

The solution was simple.

While Nancy was a hundred miles away for the next few days, Sam was working on making

Monty's divorce settlement as attractive and as generous as possible. Meanwhile, Monty planned to offer Nadine ten thousand—more than enough to get her mortgage payments current. It would be a no-interest loan "between friends"— something that wouldn't have to be repaid immediately. It would ease the pressure off her. She might even consider the gesture a sort of friendly compensation for the rough time he'd given her. Ten grand was no big deal to him—he'd recoup that in a couple of days from his stock activity.

The legal papers Wade had already drafted up were intricately worded. Nadine wouldn't know that this "loan between friends" would enable Monty to take over her property in sixty days if he wasn't repaid in full.

But he had to slip this by her casually. If Nadine felt the need to have an attorney look over the agreement, his plan would be shot.

He sincerely hoped she was desperate enough to sign the papers.

CHAPTER 28

Crouched behind the bushes across the street, Rand glared at the white Cadillac pulling up to the curb. "What's Niemus doing here?"

Harriet shrugged. "He probably wants to finish what he started last night."

"Maybe I'll have him trip on the stoop and fall flat on his—"

"You remember what I've been telling you, don't you?"

"You've been telling me a lot of things—mostly that you're turned off by all the movie trivia."

"What else?"

"Something about not hurting mortals?"

"Exactly."

"You also keep telling me this is supposed to be fun."

"You can have fun without hurting mortals."

"What's wrong with doing something interesting to an asshole like Niemus?"

"Nothing, as long as there isn't pain involved. So…do you have a plan in mind? Something suitable to our mission?"

"I thought we'd just sneak up to the back of the house and listen in. You tell me what he's doing, and I'll take it from there."

"You're not going to do anything stupid this time, are you?"

"You have *such* confidence in me."

"You have been demonstrating a sort of roguish recklessness lately."

"Me? Roguish? Reckless? How?"

"Telling her you're the grandson of the owner of the house you used to live in was pretty bad. I sincerely hope you can handle the rest of this more delicately."

"Delicate is my middle name."

"Your mother told me it was Thomas."

"You need to spend less time talking to my mother."

"That doesn't change your middle name."

"And start having a little confidence in me, all right? I can figure things out on my own. I used to be a software mogul."

"Mogul?"

"Yes. Why?"

"I thought you owned a small software company that sold—"

"How do you know so much about my company?"

"I keep telling you, I've talked to—"

"This is ridiculous. I've got work to do."

"Just don't go overboard. And do it without hurting Nadine, all right? She's been through enough."

"I'd just like to know what Niemus has in mind. I wouldn't think she'd fall for his line a second time."

"Nadine is a very rare type of person. She still carries that tiny glimmer of hope that not all men are scum. As a young girl she had the romantic illusion men were as they were portrayed in old movies—honest, always doing the right thing."

"Where'd she get *that* from?"

Harriet smiled. "Many women start out like that— especially if their father was a good man or if their first love was a pleasant experience. It takes years of heartbreak to beat them down."

"But she must have learned right off that most guys are dogs."

"Her first love substantiated her romantic illusion."

"Who was the asshole—"

Harriet's blue sapphires twinkled.

"Great. *I* was the asshole."

Harriet laughed. "As I said before, sometimes you're *so* eloquent…"

"I didn't prepare her for life at all, did I?"

"You gave her something much more precious."

"What's that?"

"Memories."

"You're not just being sappy, are you? To make me feel even *more* like a schmuck?"

"Memories such as those are rare gems. And they last forever."

CHAPTER 29

Nadine woke up on the living room couch.

How did I get here? *And what happened to—*

My God. Mr. Sherwood's grandson. He might have known Rand.

Her head throbbing again, she sat up slowly.

Was this another dream?

She fought to recall the details. Ralph coming home. The necklace. Her savings—gone. Telling Ralph to leave, that she wanted a divorce. The walk down the slope.

The sloppy-dressed, good-looking stranger with beautiful light-brown eyes and a soft, gentle voice.

"I used to live here a long time ago."

Was it possible this man knew Rand? If so, where was he?

The buzzing of the doorbell jolted her.

Maybe he'd come back to make sure she was all right.

She struggled out of the couch and, a little dizzy, hurried to the door. She'd invite him in. Then they could talk and—

Monty Niemus was standing on her front stoop.

The excitement drained from her like air from a punctured balloon. As she pulled open the door, she willed Monty to turn into Jerry. She believed in miracles, didn't she? And magic. And all sorts of other things she hadn't forgotten from childhood. If she closed her eyes and wished really hard, it just might happen...

But not this time.

"How are you feeling?"

"A little better."

"May I come in?"

She hesitated.

"Is there a problem?"

Was he serious? How could he even *ask* that after last night? "Of *course* there's a problem."

"What's wrong?"

"To be blunt, I just don't know if I can trust you."

"That's why I've come. To apologize. I feel really badly about what happened."

"You should."

"I do, believe me."

"I wish I could."

"What's stopping you?"

"You, Monty. Your reputation. The way you treat people."

"How can my reputation possibly—"

"Monty, you're a businessman—someone who uses people to get what he wants."

"That has nothing to do with what happened last night."

"Doesn't it?"

Monty suddenly looked tired. "I've done a lot of soul- searching since then. Here I am, over forty, with all sorts of *toys*...but what I really want I can't have."

"What do you want?"

186

"Someone who understands me..."

She couldn't believe he'd said that. It was the sort of cheap pickup line a man used in a bar. If he thought she was that gullible, he was way off-base. "You've got Nancy. Your wife. Remember her?"

"You know Nancy. Can you honestly say that?"

"Nancy knows what she wants. You knew that when you married her."

"She seduced me. Everyone knows that."

Nadine pushed some stray tendrils away from her eye. Monty sounded sincere, but she just wasn't in the mood for this.

"Why did you come here, Monty?"

"I thought I'd discuss my plan to help you keep the house. Since we didn't get that far at the Café, I thought maybe we could do it now." He patted his breast pocket. "I even brought along some papers that would explain everything better."

Something just occurred to her. "How did you know I wasn't working?"

He shrugged. "Stopped by the store. Artie said you weren't feeling well and decided not to come in. Which made me feel even guiltier."

She had to face facts; she did have to talk to him about this. There wasn't much time, and Ralph had made things even more impossible by exhausting her savings account.

"C'mon in." She stepped aside.

He crossed the room and took a seat on the sofa. He looked around.   "Where's Ralph?"

She'd hoped he wouldn't ask her about that. She didn't want to discuss her private life with anyone— especially Monty. But now she had no choice. "I guess I might as well tell you. We're getting a divorce."

"No!"

"He…did something I can't forgive him for."

"You're going to divorce the man because you found him at the motel last night?"

"That…wasn't the only thing he did."

Monty was nodding. "I understand."

"You do?"

He sighed. "The man's unreliable. I know that as well as you do. Hell, the whole town knows. He tries one money-making scheme after another, leaves town, comes back, leaves again, comes back, does this, does that." He shook his head. "Ridiculous."

"The bad thing is that he's really a good person, but—"

"You're about to lose your home," he suddenly blurted out, "and he waltzes into the Barnes Jewelry and buys you a customized necklace with money he took from your savings account—"

She jumped up. "How do you know about all that, Monty?"

He rose slowly; his face was flushed. He looked as if he had no idea what happened. "What…did I say?"

"You know what you said, Monty. You and Ralph have been talking, haven't you?"

"Talking?"

"Yes. You know. You say something to him, he says something back. That's how talking works, isn't it?"

He still looked confused. "Nadine, I have no idea—"

"What else have you been talking about? It wasn't a coincidence that I caught you two at the motel, was it?"

"You're getting the wrong idea—"

"Ralph is the only person who knows about my savings. Ralph and the bank. And I'm sure the bank has better ethics than tell everyone about a customer's savings account."

"I think we need to focus on how I intend to help—"

"I think we need to focus on how you know so much about Ralph and me. I'm still suspicious about why you brought me to the La-Z Inn last night. Are you going to tell me about that? Or do I have to form my own assumptions?"

Monty pulled at his shirt collar. "Your husband…he called while… while I was driving you back here."

"And how did we end up at the motel?"

"Ralph said he needed to talk to me with his realtor."

"And this couldn't be done on the phone? Or after you dropped me off?"

He still had that clueless look on his face. She could hear the gears grinding. But as smooth and as slippery as he was, he couldn't wriggle out of this one.

"Listen," he finally said. "You're in a bad position right now—"

"I know the position I'm in. I also know that you keep trying to shift the conversation away from the main topic. You've been conspiring with Ralph. I know it and so do you."

"Conspiring?"

"Scheming. Planning. Collaborating. It's in any dictionary. Everyone knows what it means."

"But…why would I—"

"You want this house badly. Once you get it, it'll make you the richest man in the county. If I didn't know better, I'd think you had something to do with that necklace Ralph bought."

He reacted as if he'd just been slapped. "Now why would I—"

"To drain me of everything—why else?" The thought of all this was making her even more furious. "I want to know why you've been talking to him and what you two have been talking about. You really have some nerve, Monty Niemus. You talk about people not understanding you while you're busy doing things behind their backs. You must think I'm stupid."

"Nadine, you've got to calm down. I know I seem guilty of everything in your eyes right now, but you've got to set that aside and think rationally. You don't have the luxury of fighting with me. You have less than three days to come up with enough money to—"

190

"I know how much time I have. I also know how much time you have before I call nine-one-one and have the police arrest you for trespassing."

His face paled. "There's…really no need to—"

The doorbell buzzed.

Monty froze.

Nadine took a deep breath. The heat shimmered down her limbs. She wanted so much to gouge out his eyes before seeing who was at the door.

Chill. Take another breath. That's it.

"Nadine?"

She hurried to the door. It was Jerry.

She was right; he hadn't been far away at all.

"I wondered where you'd gone," she said, the surge of relief warming her.

"Is this a bad time?"

She wanted to laugh. She also wanted to kiss him for showing up. "Not at all."

"May I come in?"

"Please."

The man's smile had the same calming effect on her as it had when she'd first seen him. Only then did she notice that the throbbing in her head was gone. And so was her anger.

"You again?" Monty could not hide his contempt.

"I was about to say that same thing," Jerry said, still smiling.

Monty instantly tried salvaging his superiority— clearing his throat, crossing his arms,

191

straightening. Then he gave Jerry the once-over. "I see we're still wearing the same outfit."

"Yes, but it looks to me like you've gone from Armani to something local and off-the-rack. Brooks Brothers?" Jerry tilted his head. "No, now that you're closer, I can see that the cut is different. European, most definitely. Versace? Or is it Canali? Nice threads, but still a couple of serious steps down from Armani, right?"

Nadine held back a laugh.

Monty stiffened. Instinctively he smoothed out his lapels. "How would *you* know about European fashion?"

"I know a lot of things. For instance, I can see the future."

"Really." Monty rolled his eyes. "Please proceed. I'm sure both Nadine and I will be enthralled."

Jerry closed his eyes and touched his temples with his fingertips. "Ah. In the very near future— the next few *seconds*, as a matter of fact—I can see you busting your ass to get out of this house."

Monty flinched.

Jerry approached Monty until he stood just a foot away. Although Nadine couldn't see Jerry's expression, the color quickly drained from Monty's face.

Monty backed away. He crossed the room in long strides to reach the front door. Without losing a step he yanked open the door and pushed his bulky form out of the house.

Jerry shook his head. "How about that? I was right."

"You're remarkable," she said, laughing. "How…did you do that?"

"It was nothing. I just thought, *get out of here*, and he must have heard me."

The roar of the Cadillac pierced the silence.

Nadine couldn't turn away from Jerry. His glistening brown eyes fascinated her. She thought of Rand again. Rand had similar eyes, a similar smile.

"Something wrong?"

His voice snapped her out of it.

"No. Yes. I don't know." His eyes held her fast, a shining coming from within them. "Where did you go? After you brought me back here."

"I figured you needed some quiet time. I didn't think you'd want to wake up and find a stranger in your house."

"I wouldn't have minded."

"You don't mind having strangers wandering around in your house?"

"Not you. I've got questions to ask—mostly about your grandfather."

"What about him?"

"One of his tenants was someone I knew. In the house at the corner."

"There were, I believe, three apartments in that place. The people upstairs—"

"They moved away a few years ago."

"An old man lived in the rear apartment on the first floor."

"Stanley died. Then I heard your grandfather died three or four years ago, and someone else bought the place and converted it into a private dwelling."

"That more or less takes care of it, I guess."

"Except for the ground-floor apartment facing the street."

"I can't remember who was living there. It was a long time ago—"

"A single guy. He was in his early twenties."

Jerry nodded. "That's right. It's a shame I can't remember anything about him. I only saw him once or twice. I don't even remember his name—"

"His name is Rand. Rand Powell." The mere fact that she was discussing him with someone else made her warm and dizzy.

"You okay?"

"Yes. Why?"

"You're pale. Are you going to faint again? Would you mind moving closer to the couch? You might hit your head on that end table if I don't catch you in time."

She smiled sheepishly, backing up to the couch and collapsing in it.

"What happened? You were all right a second ago."

"You...*so* remind me of...of Rand."

"Let me try a wild guess. Boyfriend?"

Boyfriend. The word seemed so inadequate. How could you sum up the man of your dreams in one word? Yet, she couldn't even call him that. "I...*wanted* him to be..."

"Let me try another wild guess. You were too young."

All she could do was nod. She could feel the tears gathering.

He sat down in the armchair. "Some things just don't turn out, I guess."

She could tell by the sadness in his eyes that he knew what she was talking about. "Can you stay?" she asked. "I'd like very much to talk to you."

"About this Rand guy?"

"About a lot of things."

"Will it help?"

"Very much."

"When I met you down by the creek, you were really depressed. Going by the idiot who was just here, I can see why. I'm sure he came over to explain why he took you to that motel, didn't he?"

She could only stare at him in amazement.

He shrugged. "Some things are kind of obvious."

"Last night was…very traumatic for me."

"I'll bet."

"I'd…like to tell you about it." It was nice being locked in his gaze. She wanted to stay there. It was a warm, cozy place—similar to her special hiding place in the basement of her parents' home when she and her sisters were kids.

"You think I'll be able to help?" he asked.

"I think you'll understand. That in itself will help."

"Is there another reason?"

The dizziness came back. "You asked if I believed in magic. Well, I do. Now more than ever."

CHAPTER 30

Steamed and confused about what had happened at Nadine's, Monty paced his home office.

Who the hell *was* that clown? And why did he keep showing up at the most inconvenient times?

This was incredible. Monty had *never* had this much trouble acquiring a piece of property. What was the problem?

He went to the desk and had another belt of Absolut from the bottle he'd brought over from the wet bar.

The one thing he couldn't understand was why he'd opened his big mouth about the necklace. He was a businessman—keeping things to himself was his stock in trade. No matter what the situation, you said only what was absolutely necessary regarding an acquisition. Letting the opposition know what cards you held was fatal. Only fools and amateurs did that.

What the hell got into me?

It had started off innocent enough, Nadine talking about her problems with Connelly, Monty sympathizing. The word "necklace" wasn't even in his head. He didn't even hear it leave his throat.

But it must have. Why else would Nadine jump out of her chair and demand to know what was going on?

197

This was almost as strange as the blackout he'd experienced when he'd left the bum at the Café and ended up at the La-Z Inn.

Strange indeed...

The phone rang. It was Connelly.

"What do *you* want?" He couldn't hold back the anger. Nothing was making sense. And he had to blame Connelly for at least *part* of it.

Because of that infernal necklace...

Silence on the other end. He'd probably scared the stupid jerk.

"Connelly? You there or what?"

"I figured I'd call and ask what's happening. Have you been to see Nadie?"

"I was there more than an hour ago."

"What happened?"

"What do you think happened?"

"Judging by your tone—"

"Connelly, do you happen to know a bum who keeps popping up whenever I'm with your wife?"

"A *what*?"

"A bum. You know. Messy clothes. Wild hair. Five o'clock shadow. Wearing a wrinkled corduroy jacket with patches and tennis shoes."

"With Nadie?"

"That's what I said."

"And he's with Nadie?"

"Is something wrong with your hearing? He's probably in his late thirties. He's been showing up whenever I'm with her. He's got a really terrific talent for making a shambles out of whatever I'm trying to do. He just showed up at the house."

"A *bum*? Hanging around *Nadie*?"

"Connelly, you're sounding like a mental case. Are you telling me you don't know anything about this idiot?"

"Yes."

"Yes what?"

"I don't know anything about this man. Where's he from?"

"How the hell should *I* know? Does it sound like I should *know* about this clown?"

"Yes. Actually, it does."

"What are you talking about?"

"He obviously knows about you, doesn't he? How else would he keep showing up when you're around?"

Connelly had a point. Beginner's luck, no doubt. "I think you might have something there." Monty sat down, had another swallow of *Absolut* and tried calming down.

"So what's he doing with Nadie?" Connelly asked.

"If I *knew* what was going on," he said tiredly, "don't you think I'd be a little calmer right now?"

"You do sound upset, now that you've mentioned it."

"Connelly, sometimes you actually show signs of an active brain cell or two."

"I wonder if I ever *have* seen him before."

"By the way, where are you?"

"I'm staying at the La-Z Inn for a few days."

"Can you afford that?"

"There's a credit card I haven't used yet."

"You're a pill. What's the APR on it?"

"Nineteen-point-seven-five. What else can I do? Sleep in my car?"

"At that rate, *I* would..."

"I figure we'll still be able to swing this deal before tomorrow evening."

"What about that real estate deal you were working on?"

"I've got until tomorrow afternoon."

"You got an extension?"

"I...pulled a string."

Monty didn't like the sound of that. With someone like Connelly, *pulling a string* couldn't possibly mean anything bright. "What exactly did you do?"

"I...hawked the necklace and gave the money to the realtor."

"That worked?"

"It got me another twenty-four hours."

Monty shook his head. Just when he thought Connelly was nothing more than a well-dressed moron lacking any sense whatsoever, he showed signs of actual brilliance. "That was good, Connelly. I'm impressed."

"Thanks, but we're still running out of time."

"We need to find out who that clown is."

"I'll go back to the house and see if I can find out."

"Will she let you back in?"

"Is that guy with her now?"

"I'm pretty sure he is."

"That might be good for us."

"How?"

"Nadie doesn't like airing out her laundry in front of someone else."

"But how will you explain why you came back?"

"I think I forgot something when I was packing up my stuff. She made me leave in a hurry, so forgetting something wouldn't be a stretch."

"Do what you can to find out who this guy is. Maybe we can get with the local law and have him arrested for vagrancy. We need to get him out of our hair."

CHAPTER 31

Her hangover completely gone, Nadine brought over two cups of coffee and set them on the kitchen table.

"What did Niemus want?" Jerry asked.

She sat facing him and picked up the creamer. "Monty wants to turn this block into a giant development. All he needs for that is this house."

"Do you want to sell it to him?"

"Not in this lifetime."

"So…he's trying to soften you up."

"Everyone knows I'm a pushover, so he probably thinks it wouldn't take much to change my mind."

"That's why he invited you to the restaurant."

"He said it was to discuss his proposal."

"Proposal?"

"He said he wants to help me keep my house."

"Why would he want you to keep the house if he needs it?"

"Monty likes to play people. He probably wants me to believe he's helping me, but he's just trying to snatch this house out from under me. He obviously thinks I won't suspect that he'd do something like that."

"What happened at the restaurant?"

"I had one glass of wine and passed out."

"Just one?"

"I usually don't drink at all. I hadn't eaten much that day. It must've gone right to my head."

"Why didn't you have much to eat?"

"Nerves, I guess."

"What's bothering you so much?"

She lowered her head. She wanted him to know what she was going through, but she also wanted to keep her secrets locked away. They were too horrible to share with anyone.

But maybe if she let them out, they'd stay out. Or maybe telling Jerry would make her feel better, somehow. She hardly knew him but felt she could trust him. She suspected that no matter what she told him, he'd understand.

"I have way too many problems. Too many to cope with."

"Why don't you just sell the house to Niemus and move?"

The mere thought of it made her sick to her stomach. Packing, taking the pictures off the walls, piling everything into a truck, driving by later on and seeing it being torn down...would tear her down as well.

"I love this place. It's my home. But they're ready to foreclose, and when they kick me out, I won't have anywhere to live. I'm kind of stuck."

"That's no reason to give up, is it?"

Despite what she'd thought, telling him her problems hadn't made her feel better. Bringing everything out in the open only made her pain much more real. But she knew she had to tell him the worst.

A tear rolled down her cheek. "I'm...dying."

***

"Get back on the other stuff." Harriet's slender white form glimmered in the kitchen archway.

He couldn't believe how callous Harriet sounded. The sapphire blues were as cold as ice. Angels were supposed to be warm, benevolent spirits, but right now Harriet was anything *but* warm or benevolent. *"The woman's dying, and you want me to—"*

"We need to hear the full story."

"Anyone ever tell you you're a butt?"

"A couple of times."

"Good. I thought it was me."

"You're also a butt--which is probably why they put us together."

Rand flinched. The way she had just said that reminded him of another circumstance.

"Something wrong?" she asked.

"Sometimes you make me feel just great."

"Feel great later. For now? The foreclosure. Her house. And, of course, her memories. Everything about her concerns us."

"I hate to sound like a pooper, but this woman's health concerns me."

"Like I said, we need to know the whole picture."

"But what about her health?"

"I'll tell you when the time comes. And by the way, you really are a pooper."

***

Nadine could tell she was frightening Jerry. He kept glancing at the kitchen doorway and frowning.

She knew how difficult it was to listen to someone else's problems. Last year a customer at the store wanted to cry on her shoulder about his wife leaving him for another man after ten years of marriage. Nadine handled the situation by ringing up his purchases in record time, smiling, and immediately directing her attention to the next customer.

She could only imagine how difficult this was for Jerry. Her story was much gloomier than her customer's.

"You seem...far away."

"I'm listening," he said, but she could tell by the way he'd shifted in his seat that he wanted to be somewhere else.

"I thought I'd feel better if I confided in someone. But somehow it just doesn't help."

"What is it?" he asked. "Cancer?"

She sniffed away another tear. "Ovarian."

"I'm *so* sorry."

She let out a deep sigh. "Things are simple when you're young. You really don't have to worry about anything. You have no sense of mortality."

"You sound like you were much happier then."

"I was."

"Tell me more about Rand."

"Are you sure you want to know?"

"It's why you asked me to stay, isn't it? Besides, you're happy when you're talking about him. All your problems seem to vanish."

"I guess I can't hide it very well, can I?"

"Did you have an affair with him?"

"It wasn't…like that."

"How was it?"

"It was almost like… a dream."

***

The first day of vacation was beautiful and clear, the sweet scent of lilacs rushing up the valley. School was out, and three glorious months of freedom lay ahead.

As was her custom to start summer vacation, Nadine awoke early. After gulping down a bowl of corn flakes she ran down the hill leading to town, where her friends would probably be hanging out at the Five'n Dime. Dorothy and Karen usually hung out there in the summer months. Dorothy liked going there because quarterback Bobby Buxton did stock work from time to time to help pay for his Firebird.

Halfway down the block she stopped cold.

Her mystery man sat in the front window of Clancy's Coffeehouse, a mug of coffee in his hand. Her previous thoughts whooshed from her head like water through an open drain.

She wanted to sneak inside but had no idea how to do it without embarrassing herself. What could she do? Plop down beside him and discuss the weather? Tell him how gorgeous he was?

Tacky, Nadie. And so gauche…

You're going to be a junior, and juniors have to be cool…

If she went in, who could she talk to? Her friends weren't there—at least she didn't think they were. She couldn't tell; the morning sun reflected

206

glare from the parked cars, making it impossible to see very far inside the storefront window.

They could be in there somewhere, couldn't they?

But what if they weren't? Surely there was someone she could talk to so she wouldn't look like a dweeb. Clancy was a nice old guy; talking to him was easy. Like most older people, he usually carried the conversation all by himself. All you had to do was look like you were listening and nod once in a while. And while you were nodding, you could have one eye focused on your guy.

She didn't drink coffee, but she did like cocoa. She could order a big mug and sit there, being cool.

As if a giant magnet was pulling her, she slipped through the open doorway.

***

"How old were you?"

Jerry poured more coffee into her mug, poured himself some, then replaced the pot.

"Fifteen." But she didn't *feel* fifteen. That was the year she stopped being a tomboy. The same year she started acting like a woman.

Jerry sat back down facing her. "Rand was an okay guy."

"You…*knew* him?" Her voice sounded like it belonged to a little girl.

"I'm only going by what my grandfather told me."

"What did he say?" she asked anxiously.

"He said Rand was never late with his rent money and didn't mind doing yard work to help out.

207

Not many renters will do that. But you wouldn't remember stuff like that, would you? It's not like you actually lived with the guy…"

You'd be surprised what I remember, she wanted to tell him.

***

Clancy's padded stool was cold and hard when she squirmed onto it that bright summer morning.

The edges of frayed duct tape covering cracks and slashes in the plastic scraped the backs of her thighs. The place was comfy and warm, and heavy with smells of coffee, toast, burnt bacon grease, and cologne. The ketchup smear on Clancy's faded white apron was shaped almost like an elongated heart.

She sat there in her blue shorts and white tee shirt that said *I AIN'T STUPID, I ALWAYS LOOK THIS WAY* in bold black letters, fifteen years old and seriously sassy, waiting for Clancy to limp over and tease her. "Makes you look like a horse," he'd say, referring to her long braided ponytail. She'd whinny and he'd let loose with his juicy cackle that always ended in a coughing fit.

Clancy hobbled over, his arthritic limp pronounced, his leathery face wrinkled with concern. Nadine supposed it was because she was looking so serious herself—which was rare for her. Clancy probably wondered if something was wrong. She'd already snuck at least twenty quick glances over the top of her menu at the man in the window seat.

208

"Seem like you got something on your mind," Clancy said.

Nadine hoped Clancy's naturally loud voice wouldn't filter over to the booth. It was important to remain anonymous. It gave her a semblance of security. Hiding behind the menu helped.

"Know Rand?"

"Who?"

"Rand Powell." Thank God Clancy had lowered his voice. "By the window. You been eyeballing the boy since you set yourself down."

Rand Powell. Nadine Powell. Rand loves Nadine.

Rand Powell loves Nadine Grove. RP hearts NG.

Ladies and gentlemen, I'd like you to meet the beautiful, happy couple, Rand and Nadine Powell...

Rand. Powell. Two quiet names. I love you, Rand. Rand darling, please come home early tonight, I've got something to tell you. Kiss me, Rand...

She wanted to rush home and write down everything that happened that morning. Her parents gave her a diary last Christmas, but she'd never wanted to put stuff in it. She preferred doing things, not writing about them. But right now, she wanted to rush back home, lock her bedroom door, remove the leather-bound journal from her dresser drawer, unlock the gold-plated clasp and write down all sorts of juicy things.

Clancy, sensing her tension, kept his voice down. He told her other things that morning—some she already knew or guessed, others she didn't. But everything Clancy said helped fashion a living, breathing man from the pristine image of the Greek god she'd created in her own adolescent mind.

Rand was about twenty-four and drove an older model emerald-green Mustang. Nadine had seen the car parked outside the driveway in the alley behind his apartment. Clancy said he ran some kind of home business but had no idea what it was. Rand always spoke, asked how you were doing. Even asked about the coffeehouse business and actually listened while you told him—as if he was really interested. Loved Clancy's coffee, always had a cup whenever he had the chance. Also liked sausage omelets—especially when you sprinkled some Colby cheese in there before you folded it over. Good tipper, too; usually stuffed a couple bucks under his plate even if all he'd had was coffee. Most folks counted their pennies, nitpicked whenever something was in their craw. Not Rand. He liked the coffee? Enjoyed his meal? There'd be a thirty percent tip shoved under his plate.

This morning, something was on the boy's mind— you could tell. Wasn't his usual friendly self, hadn't even said much when Clancy stopped by to give him his refill. Smiled, but anyone could see he didn't put much into it, just pulled back the corners of his mouth a little, left his eyes out of it totally.

Nadine listened to every word. Everything Clancy said made Rand sound like the man she'd been dreaming about ever since she'd first seen him. Nice. Quiet. Polite.

But why wasn't he married?

He wants someone like you…

She blushed at the thought. She knew she was being silly, but somehow it didn't matter. Everything about him was out of a dream—why shouldn't she think something like that if she truly believed it?

When Clancy shuffled over to the other end of the counter to give someone a coffee refill, she glanced at the window booth just to make sure Rand was still there.

The seat was empty.

CHAPTER 32

"Did you understand the situation then?" Harriet sounded concerned as she stood in front of the kitchen window.

Nadine sat in her chair, her eyes half-closed. She'd zoned out and appeared to be sleeping.

"She'd walk up and down the dirt path by the house in the mornings all summer long," Rand told her. *"I spotted her several times sitting in a lounge chair in her backyard, staring at the house."*

"And you weren't tempted to take advantage of the situation?"

"Of course I was tempted. I wasn't dead. At least, not then."

"But you didn't act on it?"

Thinking about it again after so many years was unsettling. Wrong was wrong, no matter how much time had passed. He could have no more taken advantage of Nadine than he could have pulled the wings from a butterfly. *"No,"* he said.

"What were you doing in the coffeehouse that morning?"

"Thinking."

"About what?"

"My software business."

"Clancy said he knew something was wrong."

"I never could hide things. My eyes always betrayed me."

"I've noticed. Just like now."

"How's that?"

"You're not telling me what I want to know. But they're telling me something else."

He didn't reply.

Harriet crept up behind Nadine. The sapphire blues stayed focused on him. *"Rand...why didn't you ever marry?"*

The woman sitting across the table was the reason. But Harriet didn't have to know that. *"Never met the right woman."*

"How hard did you look?"

Moving from one woman to another in an endless series of one-dimensional relationships became the summation of his existence. As a musician this lifestyle went with the territory. You traveled, performed, and met people, but formed no close attachments. Switching to software and stabilizing his existence promised a higher quality of life, but fell miserably short of his expectations.

"I didn't want to get hurt."

"What scared you off?"

"Everyone I knew or worked with was either divorced or in the process of getting one. And it was always the guy who got screwed during the divorce."

"No one ever interested you at all?" Harriet sounded surprised.

A few years earlier, he'd met a woman running a Tampa software company owned by her father. Rand bailed out early on in the relationship when he found himself so distracted that he couldn't concentrate on his work. Then he lost the company's account and never saw her again.

"There was one," he said, hoping she'd drop the subject.

"What happened?"

"Didn't feel right."

Harriet was silent.

Rand had a sip of coffee and hoped she'd finished grilling him.

"You should've pursued her," she said harshly. *"It might have worked, you know."*

"I doubt it."

Her eyes blazed. *"Stupid, stupid men..."*

"Sometimes we have to do what our gut tells us."

"How do you know something won't work if you don't even try?"

"Too late for that now, I guess."

"I'd say so," she said, a puff of hazy red emanating from her aura.

He'd obviously pissed her off. Women sure were hard to figure—even in the afterlife.

"Let's just say I screwed up and leave it at that," he said.

"I'm glad you can admit to it."

"I've always been able to admit my screw-ups."

"In that respect you're different from most men."

"In a lot of respects."

"But not *those requiring a commitment."* She turned to watch the beginnings of dusk rubbing against the kitchen window. Her hair slipped over her shoulder like a dropped curtain in a play.

CHAPTER 33

Ralph coaxed the BMW up the gravel drive, to the garage in the backyard.

Nadie's Maxima was nowhere to be seen.

He wondered if she'd gone somewhere with the bum Monty had told him about.

Then he remembered. Nadie had hitched a ride home the night before. She was probably still not feeling well, so she hadn't been able to make arrangements to pick up the Maxima. It was probably still sitting behind the Five'n Dime.

He wondered if the bum was still with her. The fact that there was no car nearby didn't mean anything; not many bums owned cars.

But it wasn't right for Nadie to spend time with a stranger when she'd just kicked her husband out of the house.

It made him suspicious.

How long had she been seeing this guy? What were they doing?

More important, what were they doing?

He sat staring at the back door, the porch, and the shuttered window. Should he knock or just barge right on in? If he knocked, he'd alert them. Nadie would have time to straighten herself out and come to the door.

It would be much better if he just barged in. It was still his house, wasn't it? They were still married. So why should he make this easier for Nadie? If she was doing something she shouldn't be doing, he could make the situation painful for her. He might even be able to use this bit of leverage to con her into postponing the divorce. Or signing Monty's papers.

That would certainly impress Niemus.

He got out of the BMW, trotted up the back steps and pushed the door open.

They were sitting at the table, drinking coffee.

Ralph instantly evaluated their expressions. They didn't seem embarrassed, just a little surprised at his sudden entrance. Both were dressed; neither wore the slightest look of guilt.

But Monty surely was right in his evaluation. The man's outfit looked like he'd picked it up at some bargain basement—patches, wrinkles and split seams. His hair was a mess, and he badly needed a shave.

So what was he doing with Nadie?

"What are you doing here?" She sounded more curious than upset.

"I...forgot something." He couldn't take his eyes off the man. It had nothing to do with the outfit; it was his eyes. They were steady and very intense. Ralph had the feeling the man was actually reading him to find out the *real* purpose for this surprise visit.

"This is Jerry," Nadie said. "Jerry Sherwood. Jerry, my husband Ralph."

"Hello."

The man nodded and continued to stare.

"What did you forget, Ralph?" Nadie asked.

"Something I left...in the bedroom."

216

"No problem." Nadie turned back to her visitor. "When I saw that he'd gone," she said, "I didn't know what to do."

"I haven't been gone *that* long," Ralph said, forcing a grin.

"We're not talking about you." Nadie was still looking at her visitor.

Ralph's grin quickly dissolved.

"I'll bet you were surprised," Jerry said to Nadie.

She shrugged. "Surprised wasn't the word. Like I said, the whole thing started out strange—"

"You won't mind if I go upstairs for a moment, will you?" Ralph asked.

Nadie still didn't take her eyes off her visitor. She didn't seem to be aware of anyone else in the room. "Go ahead, Ralph." Then, to her visitor: "It was all so unreal…"

"Unreal?" Ralph asked.

She finally turned in his direction. Her expression was one of contempt. "Jerry and I are reminiscing."

"You two *know* one another?"

"We have a mutual friend."

This could be the perfect opportunity to find out about the man. He and Monty needed to know what was going on. "You live here?" he asked Nadie's visitor.

"No." The man picked up his coffee cup.

So much for *that* bit of information…

Reminiscing. Having a mutual friend. The man didn't live here.

So why was he here? And where did he live?

"Ralph, do what you have to do."

"I'll bet you weren't quite ready for something like that, were you?" Jerry said to Nadie.

"Not at all."

"Ready for what?" Ralph asked.

Neither replied. They were ignoring him.

Damn, he thought, tiny bubbles of heat scurrying up his limbs. *This is my house and that's my wife...and* I'm *the intruder*.

But he couldn't very well cause a scene without it backfiring.

"I'll just...go on upstairs and have a look," he said.

Nadie said, "I wish I could make you understand how unreal the whole situation was—"

"Oh, I understand," Jerry said.

"But it's one of those things you can't understand unless you've been through it yourself."

"I've actually been through something similar..."

Upstairs, Ralph dialed Monty's number.

Monty answered immediately. "What's going on?"

"You're right, Mr. Niemus."

"About what?"

"Two things. One, the man's a bum. And two, we need to do something to get him out of the picture."

"That didn't take long."

"I think Nadie's planning something with the guy."

218

"What did she say?"

"It's not what she said, it's how they were talking."

"What were they talking about?"

"It's not *what* they were talking about, it was *how* they were talking. It sounded really strange—as though they were making it up as they went along."

"They obviously didn't want you overhearing."

"Exactly."

"You may be right, Connelly. They could be planning something. Possibly some sort of a squeeze play with the house."

"That means we've got to outthink them."

Niemus chuckled. "In that case, they're in for a rude awakening. I'm way the hell out of their league."

CHAPTER 34

After Ralph left, Jerry joined Nadine on the living room couch.

She didn't know why she felt so relieved. Maybe it was because she hadn't liked the intrusion and had been on edge all the while Ralph was upstairs. And even though the intruder was her husband, he'd interrupted them while they were talking about something very close to her heart. And despite the feeling of contentment she had in Jerry's presence, she'd reacted to Ralph's interruption in anger and frustration.

"So that was your husband," Jerry said, and she could tell by his tone that he was disappointed.

Nadine sighed. "I'm afraid so." She felt badly for saying it like that, but she couldn't help it. She was ashamed of Ralph, of herself for marrying him and of what they'd made of their marriage.

"He never did say if he found what he was looking for."

"No. He didn't, did he?"

"He wasn't up there very long, either."

"It makes me wonder why he came back." She suspected that he'd try and apologize one last time, but reconsidered when she found Jerry with her, and made up the story of forgetting something just to avoid embarrassment. "Tell me something."

"Sure."

"Why'd you marry him?"

She shrugged. "He asked me."

"That's all it took?"

"At the time."

It was a rough period in her life. She'd just spent several months trying to divide her parents' estate equally among herself and her two sisters—which didn't turn out very well, no matter what she did. She also had problems when Doc Adams got sick and piled more work on her at the office because he didn't trust anyone else. She'd met Ralph at the local branch, where she was taking courses at night. She liked the way he made her laugh, the way he made her feel, and thought it would be a good match.

She knew Jerry wanted to ask more but might consider the subject too delicate. Or maybe he'd been there, too. He had said that he understood. That he'd been through something similar.

She believed him. A kind, sensitive man was hiding beneath the rumpled clothes and the five-o'clock shadow. She could also see a sadness mixed among the shadows in his sparkling, light-brown eyes.

This man obviously knew hurt and sorrow.

"Tell me the rest of the story," he said. "Were you disappointed to find out about Rand?"

"This'll sound strange, but it bummed me out. It's like on Christmas morning, when you're opening your presents. You've been staring at them for days, wondering what's inside. Every time you pass the tree you stop and spend a couple of minutes looking at them, even picking them up, hoping your X-ray vision will help you see through the wrappings. You might even know what's inside. But when everything's unwrapped and the mystery's over, it's a let-down."

"So you were disappointed when you found out Rand was a human being."

"It was the little girl in me. But the other part— the woman I'd suddenly become—was *far* from disappointed."

"What did you do when you discovered he'd left the coffeehouse?"

"I ran outside and followed him up the hill. I kept my distance, ready to dive behind a bush if he turned around. I was gonna stop when I reached his house, sit on the step and re-lace my tennis shoe, or take it off and look for a pebble. But when I turned the corner, he was standing on the porch, smiling at me."

"What happened?"

"He said, 'Hi.'" Her voice dropped to a whisper.

"And what did *you* say?"

"I started running and tripped over my own two feet."

***

"What did you *do, Romeo?"* Harriet asked from the armchair.

It was years since Rand thought about that Saturday. Years since he'd relived the incident in his mind.

"What do you think? I went to help her."

Even after all these years he clearly remembered the cold stab of guilt when he saw her

222

fall, the flood of heat thundering through him when he heard her thump onto the pavement. Even though the deed had long since passed, he hated himself once again for making it happen.

***

"Are you all right?" Rand knelt on one knee while she pulled herself into a sitting position. "I didn't mean to—"

"I'm...okay." Her cheeks were red. Dirt darkened her forearms, left knee, and the seat of her shorts. A stray leaf from one of the buckeyes lining the walk clung to her ponytail. It took every bit of self-control he could find to refrain from brushing it off.

He took her hand. Feeling the heat in it, the trembling, he tried to ignore the stirring in his limbs from her touch. Her big blue eyes were on him; they said she liked him and liked holding his hand. But his only concern was that she'd fallen and had hurt herself. Her right knee was covered with tiny red bubbles glistening in the morning sun.

"Can I take you to the hospital? You're bleeding."

"I'm fine. I always hurt myself sooner or later." She jerked free and ran down the street. She stopped for one moment to look at him before running up the stairs of her front porch.

***

"He was *so* sweet," Nadine said, smiling.

The memories were as bright and as clear as ever. "So concerned I was okay. But I was *so* embarrassed, I couldn't get away fast enough."

223

"I'm sure he was, too," Jerry said softly.

"If he was, he didn't show it."

"He probably didn't want you to know."

"You're probably right. True gentlemen are like that, aren't they?"

"I guess so..."

"He acted that way the next time I saw him. About two weeks later, when I was walking home— I might have been at Dorothy's place. Tommy Ray Simons, the town bully, jumped out of the bushes across the street from my folks' place. Tommy Ray was twenty years old and had flunked out of school the year before. He was always pushing us around.

"Anyway, Tommy Ray really scared me. I was backing up and getting ready to run, but he kept yelling at me—which scared me even more. Before I realized it, I was standing in the middle of the street and a sportscar was coming right at me. I didn't even realize how close it was until someone grabbed me by the waist, picked me up, and set me back down on the sidewalk. I still had no idea what was going on, and when I turned around and saw Rand

(*the overpass*)

standing there,

(*reaching out*)

a frightened look on his face—"

"Go on."

She was silent.

Confusion set in. Last night. There was something weird about what happened last night.

The overpass. Had it been real? Had she really been there?

Or had she imagined it all along?

Maybe she *did* trip and fall after she turned away from Ralph and Monty. Maybe she hit her head and immediately made up a dream based on the event with Tommy Ray, which somehow brought Rand back—

"Nadine? Something wrong?"

***

"She's remembering last night," Harriet said.

"I figured it might be something like that," Rand said. *"What do I do?"*

"Wait until it passes. She can't possibly put the two together."

"I hope you're right."

"By the way, how is it that you showed up when you did?"

"I just happened to be coming out of the Burger King when I saw her that morning."

"How did you manage to get close enough to save her life?"

He was leaving the place when he saw her down the street, backing up from the husky moron with the buzz cut and the crazy eyes. A jolt of anger stabbed him, and before he realized it, he was rushing down the street in

her direction.

"I don't know. I guess I was just lucky."

"You wanted her, didn't you? Despite all you've told me."

He just sighed.

225

"It's written all over your face," she said.

The guilt, dormant after so many years, flooded back.

"Every time I saw her," he said.

***

Nadine ran her hands through her hair.

That sure was weird. It was almost like what happened last night had blended in with what happened fifteen years ago, making it impossible to tell what was real and what wasn't.

"Are you all right?" Jerry asked.

"It's so strange, talking about this after all these years."

"I can imagine."

"It was…like a dream. Sometimes I tell myself I imagined the whole thing. I even had a similar dream last night, when I woke up in Monty's car at the motel. That was even stranger than what happened with Rand."

"Dreams can play tricks on you, all right."

"But just when I try analyzing it, a lot of things tell me it actually happened."

"Rand saved your life. That certainly elevated his status with you even more."

"After Clancy told me about him that morning, I realized he was just another guy. But when he saved my life later on…" The warmth came back, and she knew instantly what was real. "He went right back up there in the clouds and stayed there."

"He just happened to be close by. Anyone else might have done the same thing."

She knew better. No one could convince her that what Rand did was anything but extraordinary. "I was only a block or so from the Burger King when Tommy Ray jumped out of the bushes. A few senior jocks were in the front parking lot, revving their engines. Any one of them could have reacted, but they were too busy trying to impress one another. I recognized the sportscar after it passed. He was a friend of theirs and was probably just showing off. He probably didn't even see me."

"What happened after Rand pulled you out of the way?"

"The next thing I knew, I was sitting on the grass off the curb. I must have passed out—I don't remember. Something like that does a serious job on your nerves. It was probably shock, I don't know. But I do remember looking into Rand's eyes and feeling happier than I ever felt before. And I could tell by the way he was looking at me that he felt the same way."

***

"I'm sorry, Rand."

Harriet's sapphire blues were cloaked in sadness. She slumped in the armchair, a pale version of Mary in Michelangelo's *Pieta. "I didn't know the whole story."*

He managed a weak smile. For some reason this wasn't as horrible as he suspected it would be. The last fifteen years had evidently taken some of the bite out of it. And despite his initial reluctance to come back into Nadine's life, he was experiencing genuine warmth by reliving these wonderful memories with the very woman who had created them.

"Well, now you do."

"I wasn't aware of your true feelings. I'd assumed she was the one smitten and that you being the kind of man you are, shrugged it off."

"There was something very special about her. I tried resisting, but she grabbed my heart and held on."

"When I asked why you never married, did you tell me the whole story?"

"I moved a thousand miles away. What does that tell you?"

"You moved away because of Nadine?"

"I needed to get away."

"What was wrong with Wheeling? You had business contacts there, didn't you?"

"Yes."

"But you didn't move there."

"No."

"So, you moved to Florida and never looked back."

"I wanted to come back and see what had become of Nadine. I thought that if I waited five or ten years, she'd be a better age and things would be more favorable. But part of me was afraid to."

"Why not?"

"I don't know if I actually wanted it to happen. It was my cynical side taking over, convincing me that the best things in life were merely dreams. Life hadn't been kind up to that point— why should it change? As a musician I had a lot going for me, but

society had turned its back on my music. Eventually it turned back around—as things usually do—but by the time my music was popular again I'd found a different career and no longer had the desire. I guess that was the way I felt about coming back here. Otherwise, I would have bought a plane ticket."

"The time wouldn't have been right."

"With my luck, I would've probably come back when she was marrying Mr. Smooth. That would have done wonders for my ego."

"I can only imagine how difficult it was, saving her life on the overpass."

"It wasn't difficult at all."

"But if you'd let her fall . . ."

"That wasn't even an option."

Harriet smiled. *"You're very special, Rand."*

"I'll bet you say that to all the dead guys."

CHAPTER 35

The Mustang Saloon on South Chestnut was doing its usual business that evening.

The thundering juke caused the small, debris-cluttered rear lot to vibrate loudly with screechy fiddles and the usual country twang. The floods blazed, highlighting the tricked-out pickups lined up along the dirty block wall.

Monty Niemus sat behind the wheel of the Caddie, performing a drum roll on the steering wheel. Beside him, Connelly hunched over, chewing a fingernail.

Monty kept the windows closed to keep the stink—and the ear-splitting twang—from seeping in. He hated coming here and would have preferred leaving this matter to someone reliable. But the time element was crucial; he didn't have the luxury of making the necessary phone calls and waiting to see who was available. By the time the night was over he was going to have to take the Caddie in for a wash and wax and have Roberto check the tire treads to see what Monty had picked up coming to this dive.

The Mustang was the local armpit. Monty had tried buying out the owners several times, but the hick element was more than he could contend with. Too many losers came here because they were too stupid and too poor to go anywhere else. But if it kept them out of the places Monty frequented, then it was worth it to have it here even if it was only a block across from Monty's office and the reek

230

drifted over when the wind was blowing the wrong way.

It would help considerably if they could have the area cleaned up occasionally. Broken glass, beer bottles, candy wrappers and used condoms, strewn everywhere, made the area look like downtown Beirut.

Yep, he'd have to take the Caddie in first thing tomorrow.

"You sure we've got to do things this way?" Connelly asked.

Monty wanted to reach over and slap the boy across the back of the head. As smart as Connelly thought he was, he hadn't yet been indoctrinated into the seamy aspect of wheeling and dealing. Sometimes you just had to cut corners—which often meant getting dirty. But when you had money, you could usually keep yourself from soiling your own hands.

"You have a better solution?"

"It just seems so…so mob-like."

"What's bugging you, Connelly?"

"This whole thing." He shifted in his seat. "It reeks of the *Sopranos*. Or *Dukes of Hazzard*, even. I've never done anything like this before. What if a cop shows up? What if someone talks? What if something goes wrong and—"

"Calm down, dammit."

"But—"

"You've got to think things out when you're working a major deal. Sometimes the pieces don't naturally fit into one another. It's like a puzzle, only

231

when you're dealing with people—especially clowns who get in your way—you've got to cut and shape the pieces to fit your purpose."

"But what we're doing. Isn't it…illegal?"

Connelly was an idiot. He wouldn't have said that if he wasn't. He obviously had accidentally stumbled onto a book of the world's greatest lines to coax a fox like Nadine to the altar.

"A lot of things are illegal. In fact, I know several businessmen who refuse to do anything illegal, and you know what? With that sort of mindset, they'll never achieve the degree of success I've achieved. No one really makes it unless he's prepared to do whatever it takes to reach his goal. If you've got a better way, I'd like to hear it. You know *why* I'd like to hear it?"

"Why?"

"This isn't exactly my favorite area. I'd much rather be enjoying a lobster dinner in a high-class Wheeling restaurant right now. I'd even rather be at church, dozing off while the Reverend Winthrop is chattering away in an attempt to redeem my soul. I'd rather be anywhere than here, as a matter of fact. Sitting in the tub, clipping my toenails would be preferable to this. I hate bringing the Caddie within a mile of this rat trap. Because of it, I'll have to take her in tomorrow morning, get her washed and waxed, and have them check the tires for broken glass, tacks, and God only knows what else we may have picked up. And it makes me want to take a shower as well."

"Then why are we even here?"

"It has to be done. We're running out of options and time. I need your wife's house. There's someone standing in our way, and I don't know what else to do. Got it?"

"You sure we'll be able to…to *do* this?" Connelly asked.

"I've done things like this before. It's not as difficult as you might think."

"You've…had people beaten up before?"

"Connelly, grow up. You're over thirty. It's time to climb out of the crib and open your eyes. You want something really good in this life, there's an excellent chance someone else is going to want the same thing. You have one of two options. You can step aside, smile politely and let him have what you want, or smile politely and do what needs to be done to get him the hell out of your way. Which is it going to be?"

Connelly didn't reply.

"I stand to make a fortune when I appropriate your wife's house. The only obstacles are your wife, of course, and that clown she's with. If I can get the clown out of our way, I'll stand a much better chance of conning her into handing over the house. Simple enough?"

Two large, rough-looking characters staggered out of the bar. One wore tight jeans, motorcycle boots and a leather vest. The other a do-rag, black tank top, jeans, and black cowboy boots. The one wearing the do-rag was firing up a cigarette as they crossed the lot.

"Showtime." Monty reached into his pants pocket. When his hand came out, a thick wad of bills was trapped in it. "Now you're gonna see what people will do for a little pocket money." He eased the window down, wincing at the sourness in the air. Then he cleared his throat. "Gentlemen! You have a minute?"

The two stopped, stared, then wandered cautiously over to the Caddie..

The one wearing the vest pulled the cigarette out of his mouth and blew the smoke in Monty's direction. "Ya talkin' to us, Jack?"

Monty waved the smoke away. "You two doing anything right now?"

The other scowled and said, "What's it to ya?"

Monty held up the wad trapped in his right palm. "How would you like to earn five hundred bucks for one minute's work?"

"Who do we gotta kill?" they both said, grinning.

CHAPTER 36

At eleven o'clock Rand got up from the couch. Nadine looked all done in. He knew she'd been through enough for one day.

"I should be going."

Nadine rubbed her eyes. She glanced at the clock on the wall above the television. "Goodness...I've had you here for *hours*."

"They went by fast."

She searched his face. "But I feel so guilty... We were going to talk about your grandfather, but all I did was whine—"

"I wouldn't have stayed if I didn't want to."

She smiled.

"She likes you, Rand." Harriet drifted over to the door.

"If she knew who I really am—or was..."

"Let's not go there."

"Will I...see you again?"

"Most definitely." Rand tried not to notice her smell, her closeness. He couldn't quite understand how he'd been able to talk to her at all. His protective covering hid him from her, making him anonymous. The covering—as well as the passage of time—made him feel anonymous as well.

But it didn't change the fact that she was Nadine...and he'd miraculously returned to her life.

"I'd like to thank you again." Her beautiful eyes held him fast. The familiar urge that had been dead for so many years stormed through him. He

235

struggled to concentrate on the present. Everything had taken place a long time ago, to two very different people in a very different world.

"It was nothing," he said.

She took a step closer. "It was to *me*..."

This time her closeness was impossible to ignore. Harriet remained off to his left, jabbing an impatient thumb at the door.

"Well, good night." He pulled open the door and slipped out into the cool clear night.

***

As Rand edged down the walk barely feeling the pressure of his tennis shoes on the hard concrete, he drifted into a filmy trance.

His consciousness was stuck between past and present. With each step, the present dimmed before finally dissolving into the darkness of the night.

The big apartment house jutted out from the knob of the hill one street down. He wanted to get some work done in his office before he went to bed. He wondered if Nadine was peeking at him from her living room window...if she'd be walking past the house the next morning in her blue and white striped bikini...

No. Not the right season for the bikini. It was already fall—she'd probably be wearing—

"We're being followed, Rand."

Harriet's voice jerked him back into the present. It took him several seconds to get his bearings. *That's right. Harriet. I'm dead. How could I forget something like that?*

"What do you mean, followed?" he whispered.

"What do you think I mean? Followed, as in hunt. Or track. Stalk might even be appropriate. Someone's behind us, walking in the same direction."

"Behind us?"

"Snap out of it." Even in the dark he could see the alarm on her face. "Where are you?"

"I'm okay now. Sorry."

"Good. Now…what are we talking about?"

"We're being followed."

"Someone just got out of a pickup truck down the street."

When Rand stopped to turn, Harriet touched his arm. "Don't look. Something tells me we'd better play along."

"Maybe someone's coming home late."

"I don't think so. Whoever got out of that truck has been watching us."

"I wonder who it is."

"I really can't say yet."

"Please find out, okay?"

"Give me a minute."

"What should I do while you're sniffing around?"

"Keep walking. And act clueless."

"You mean like a high-fashion model? Or politician?"

"You're on the right track."

"I can't guarantee anything. I *was* a software mogul."

Harriet shook her head.

Rand said, "You gonna start that again?"

"Why don't you just say you ran a small software company and leave it at that?"

"It wasn't *that* small."

"However big it was, you weren't a mogul."

"Anyway, I was known for my brilliance. Acting clueless was never something I was able to do very well."

"Make believe you're involved with a woman who really likes you. In that respect, you've got clueless down perfectly."

"You can be really *cold*," he said.

She'd already faded into the night.

***

Her white form reappeared beside him only moments later. "There are two men back there. Apparently Niemus gave them five hundred dollars to beat you up."

"Not very sporting, is it?"

"I keep telling you he isn't a nice man."

"So what do I do?"

"It's very simple. You get rid of them. Humanely, of course."

"There's always a catch, isn't there?"

"That still gives us plenty of leeway."

"I wonder where he found them."

"They reek of whiskey, cigarettes, and sweat. I imagine he found them at the local bar."

"That's downright insulting."

"You'd rather Niemus had hired expensive, well-dressed thugs?"

"That doesn't sound very sporting, either."

"He obviously wants to make sure you don't go back to Nadine. These two are big, stupid, and—worst of all—drunk."

"Do you think Nadine is safe?"

"Niemus won't try anything else with her until he knows you're out of commission."

"Any suggestions?"

"I'll let you figure something out. Just don't—"

"Damage this covering. Yes. I know."

"Or—"

"Hurt them. I get you."

"I'm *so* glad your memory's still on the ball."

"You're not gonna leave me again, are you?"

Harriet shrugged and tried to look innocent.

"Any way you can stop being so damned cute?"

"I thought you liked cute."

"In moderation. Right now, I need something more practical."

"Such as?"

"A hint."

"Like I said before, this is your ballgame."

"What if I strike out?"

"We're hoping you will, so you'll learn from the experience."

"Then let's get this over with. Something tells me I'm gonna have my hands full tomorrow."

"Sometimes you're *so* perceptive." Then she was gone.

At the corner, bugs circling the streetlight tapped against the glass dome. The faint malodor of stale beer emanating from the crushed cans lying near the curb added bitterness to the air.

239

Sudden movement rushed at him from behind. A huge presence approached him from the right. The one behind him grabbed him in a viselike grip, pinning Rand's arms to his sides. The whiskey-cigarette miasma enveloped him.

"What's up, guys?" he asked. "Out for a romantic stroll in the moonlight?"

The other came at him dead-on, something glinting in his hand. Brass knuckles. Harriet was going to be pissed.

The arm came back. And stopped.

The two men quickly froze into a stony stillness. Rand was reminded of the traffic on I-70 the previous night.

Exhaling, he bent at the knees, squirming out of the first thug's grip. He stepped away.

The two remained frozen—the first thug gripping empty air, his buddy ready to deliver a pulverizing blow.

"Admiring your handiwork, I see." Harriet drifted over.

"These two need a bath," he said, sniffing. "Big-time."

"What's that in his hand?"

"Brass knuckles."

"What's it for?"

"You don't get around much, do you?"

She pursed her lips. "I spent too much time in finishing school, learning all about men like you. What's it for?"

"To rearrange my facial features." He pried the weapon from the thug's tight grip.

"That's not very nice." Harriet frowned.

"You're right. Someone's liable to get hurt."

"But tell me…why would you think I'd know about something like that?"

"Everyone knows about brass knuckles."

"My parents didn't feel the need to inform me about such interesting things."

"That's funny. You don't *seem* like a sheltered princess."

"That's a matter of opinion. So…where do you recommend they have their bath?"

"I think they need to cleanse their souls first."

"Spoken like a true benevolent spirit." Harriet nodded her approval. "I'm proud of you. Let's get this finished. It'll be morning soon."

He stepped back and patiently waited for mortal time to resume.

***

Buster hauled off and let the mark have it right in the kisser.

But at the last moment he saw his fist connect with Ride's left cheek. Ride gasped, dropping to his knees, and grabbing his jaw.

"What the *hell?*" His head buzzing, Buster spun around. The mark was standing behind him, a smile on his face, Buster's brass knuckles lying in the other man's open palm. "How the *fuck*—"

"I guess I move slightly faster than you two." The mark pocketed the knuckles. "Nasty toy. You could actually hurt someone with this."

241

Ride coughed up blood and hawked it out. It slapped the pavement. "You asshole...what the fuck do ya think you're doin'?"

The mark said, "You guys have had too much to drink."

Buster couldn't imagine what happened. One moment he was ready to turn the mark into bloody pulp; the next moment Ride was on his knees, coughing up blood.

"I think you could use a few minutes in church," the mark said with a smile.

"*What*?"

"You know. That big stone building two streets down? It's got a steeple with a bell in it? Pews inside? A cross? An atmosphere of peace and tranquility? I think you two need to spend some time there. You've been bad, you know. Real bad. Your mothers should be ashamed."

Buster hadn't been to church since he was a kid. What the hell was in that rotgut they'd sold them at the Mustang?

Ride was standing now, swaying, still holding his jaw and coughing up blood. His eyes were wet. "You son of a—"

"Temper, temper." The mark was shaking his head. "Go on, now. Spend a little time in church. It'll do you both a lot of good."

"*Church*?" Ride practically lost his balance.

"That's what the man said," Buster said.

"What about...the money?" Ride asked.

The mark said, "I'm sure Monty won't miss it. But since you brought it up, I think it would be a

242

real good thing to drop it in the donation box on your way inside."

Without a word, they turned and staggered down the walk.

THE LAST DAY

CHAPTER 37

Huddled in the shower stall, Nadine hardly noticed the warm water cascading down on her.

Everything in her life had suddenly changed. Through a strange sequence of events, she believed her existence might not be so hopeless after all—that things might possibly even turn around.

Dabbing at her wet hair with a light-blue bath towel, she approached the mirror. She picked up a comb from the wicker basket on the counter and forced it through the honey-blond tangles. Her reflection made her stiffen. Her pulse thumping, she dropped the towel.

What was this?

Her eyes were playing tricks. She might still have sleep in them.

She leaned closer for a better look.

The crow's feet she'd been carrying around the last couple of years. Those ugly slivers fanning out from the corners of her eyes that had literally taken over.

They were *gone*.

Not all of them, but enough to make a big difference.

What was going on?

Gently she touched her skin with her fingertips. It was smooth and blemish-free.

Braced against the sink, she held her breath, expecting the creases to return. She just knew she was imagining this. She just knew that at any moment, they'd be making a return appearance.

But they didn't. They'd vanished.

Each time she searched for some shred of logic to explain this, Jerry's image flashed brightly in her head, with Rand Powell's face immediately following.

Why did she have this nagging suspicion her dream lover from fifteen years past could somehow be involved in any of this inexplicable weirdness?

She drifted into a hazy trance while groping for her underthings from the dresser drawer. Going through the motions, she moved as if on air...as if she'd somehow shifted from reality to fantasy.

Why did everything feel so different?

Her existence, which until recently seemed so hopeless, had become a series of strange, unfathomable mysteries. Through her bedroom window, an eerie golden glow flickered from the morning sun. The sky appeared as pure as the sea. The cool air drifting in through the cracked window held the same sweetness as orange blossoms.

What on earth was happening to her?

Why weren't things so bleak anymore?

CHAPTER 38

The clinking of forks and knives, the clatter of plates and dishes, and the soft mutterings of early morning customers filled the large open room of the St. Clairsville Breakfast Nook.

The Nook had always been one of Monty Niemus' favorite breakfast stops. His first choice, in this case, for this morning's celebration.

Breakfast—eggs Benedict, pancakes, toast, marmalade, and the terrific chicory coffee the place was known for—served as a symphony for the palate. The décor and the excellent service also impressed him. Even the view from his corner window booth provided a vista of fresh autumn color from the trees embellishing the steep hill above Interstate 70.

Monty was confident that he'd spent his money wisely last night. The two thugs he'd paid certainly were more than qualified for the task. One call to the Barnes Hospital would tell him if someone had been brought in the night before as the result of a terrible beating.

But such a call should be unnecessary. When you paid two thugs good money to beat up someone, you knew they wouldn't let you down.

Which left him free to conclude his business with Nadine without interruptions.

His cell buzzed.

He dug it out of his jacket pocket and checked the number on the display. Connelly… Hopefully, a progress report…

He switched it on. "Anything happening at the house?"

"I haven't seen any activity, Mr. Niemus."

"How long have you been watching?"

"I've been across the street since six o'clock this morning."

"And you've seen nothing?"

"Not a thing."

"I'd say off-hand that we've just rid ourselves of one irritating bum."

"Looks like it. So what's next?"

"I have some business to tend to after breakfast. Then I'll check in on your wife and this time we won't be disturbed when I give her my proposal."

"I have a few things to do myself."

"Such as?"

"I need to go to the bank and use up the rest of her savings account."

"I didn't think she had much left."

"There's still enough for me to buy a new outfit."

"You're buying *clothes* with the rest of her money?"

"I'm a little miffed that she threw me out yesterday."

"Connelly, sometimes you amaze me."

"I just think having her pay for a few bounced checks might make me feel a little better about this whole thing."

***

Inside the bank, Harriet sat on top of the writing table.

Less than two feet away, Nadine's husband leaned over, scratching out a check. His aftershave was even more overpowering than Niemus' expensive brand.

It was a shame Rand wasn't here. His appearance would cause this man much well-deserved anguish.

But it wouldn't be wise for him to reappear this soon. Nadine's husband would alert Niemus and compromise this mission. Harriet wanted the two men to get on with their plans. If they thought they were safe, they'd do what was necessary for their own ruin.

That was the good thing about opportunists— they nearly always turned out to be their own worst enemies. All that was needed now was some tweaking.

Connelly wasn't nearly as corrupt as Niemus but well on his way. If he spent more time with Niemus he would soon be a carbon copy, which the world—or at least in this case, Barnes—didn't need.

***

Ralph couldn't help noticing the cute teller peeking at him while he stood in line.

A little young, but she definitely knew how to dress. And she had that slim, coltish figure he liked so well. He guessed she'd only graduated from high school a couple of years earlier and was probably

248

working here so she could hook up with someone rich.

That's what the young chicks wanted nowadays. And in just a few hours, Ralph would be that someone. Not that he'd want someone that young, of course. He was thirty-two—there was no need to rob the cradle when he'd soon have his pick.

"May I help you?"

"I need to cash this check."

"One moment." She took it, looked at it, flipped it over and frowned. "Sir, is this your wife's signature?"

"Actually, my soon to be *ex*-wife." It wouldn't hurt to start advertising, would it? Especially when there were so many nice-looking babes in the work force. Like this one, although she didn't seem as friendly as she was a moment ago. She kept studying the back of the check, her screen, then at him.

He'd trained himself to duplicate Nadie's signature more than a year ago. He was so good at it, in fact, that he'd been pulling out small amounts of money whenever he'd felt the need. And no one had been the wiser.

But something was wrong. The teller wasn't clicking any keys...or opening any drawers...or pulling out any bills.

"What's wrong?"

"It's...your wife's signature."

"What about it?"

"It...isn't hers."

The back of his neck buzzed. "That's crazy. I was right there when she signed it…"

The teller slid it across the counter. He reached beneath the cage and grabbed it.

What the *hell*?

He couldn't believe it.

The name on the check was spelled

N-A-D-E-E-N C- O-N-L-I-E.

CHAPTER 39

Drifting silently into Montgomery Niemus' lush home office, Harriet touched down in the center of the Turkish rug.

The room was large, the walls paneled. One section was lined with hardbound books and sculptures of naked women. Elegant French doors overlooked a flower garden. A large, framed oil painting of a smiling, exquisitely dressed Monty Niemus dominated one wall.

Niemus came in, plopped down behind the huge mahogany desk, propped his feet up and belched loudly. He reached into his trouser pocket, pulled out a breath freshener, opened his mouth wide and sprayed. Harriet caught a strong whiff of peppermint. Niemus picked up the telephone from the desk. He wedged the receiver in the crook of his neck and dialed. He was admiring his manicured nails as he spoke.

The expression on his face was much like that in the painting.

"Abner Hargrove, please. This is Monty Niemus…Yes, I'll wait…"

He began whistling softly.

A moment later, he stopped whistling. "Abner, how's business? Fine, just fine. I was just wondering if I could stop by this afternoon. Three o'clock? Dandy. Why, the Connelly house. Eight-twenty-five, Elm. There's a foreclosure on it, I understand…"

The man's hair, the ring-adorned hands—everything about him was nasty and unpleasant. Almost foul.

It would be a pleasure to change this wicked mortal into a raving lunatic.

But she couldn't. An angel's powers were limited. Besides, angels just didn't do things like that.

Anyway, her role was minor. She was under strict orders to remain in the background. Rand must earn his place. It was up to her to see that he developed into the angel he was destined to be. She hadn't been mentoring long but realized she needed to be more patient, let her apprentice analyze things for himself. This had always worked in the past, but she knew this assignment would be the most difficult of her career.

She'd fought hard to stay out of this from the beginning, but they remained as obstinate as always, their wings and robes and long hair completely unruffled by her hysteria. It was necessary for her to be the mentor. Rand was their first and only choice for this mission in Barnes, Ohio. And her personal history made her part just as essential. Her involvement was just as personal as Rand's was with Nadine.

Intervening was crucial if it was to be wrapped up quickly and efficiently. And considering the types she and Rand were dealing with, the *only* way of handling this was to finish quickly and efficiently.

The fact that Montgomery Niemus was a disgusting creature in a stunning wardrobe made things even more distasteful. It bought and sold people's dreams and used the profits to obtain comfort and happiness for itself. It didn't care about anyone else, didn't consider a person's tears or anguish, and slept soundly at night.

It was a monster.

Niemus replaced the phone, then swiveled around in his chair to admire the painting. As he did so, he carefully patted his hair.

His thoughts rang loud and clear.

Nadine, in just a few hours you're going to give me your house. And you won't even know you did it.

Harriet crept over to the slimy creature. Its hair was *oh so* tempting. It was apparent how much care and money it took to keep it looking that way. How amusing it would be to mess it up.

Rumble...

Niemus turned in his seat to face the French doors. It had been so sunny moments ago. And there hadn't been rain in the forecast. Perhaps a freaky autumn storm was on its way...

Harriet raised her face toward the ceiling. A slim golden tunnel extending to the heavens above flickered brightly, like gleaming jewels.

The abrupt reminder rippled down the tunnel: RAND...

Yes. Despite her personal feelings, she must let him work his newly acquired magic.

But this was difficult. It had been torture, coaxing him from his broken body, pulling him into her sphere. Being close to him again, penetrating his innermost thoughts... Noting how important the protective covering hiding his face really was.

But the covering couldn't hide his inner self. The face was different, but it was Rand underneath. Even now she couldn't believe she'd kept up the charade this long.

This was the last day of their mission. Very shortly she'd see his true face again. And he'd see hers.

First things first. Stick to the job, then worry about what happens...

Considering the situation and the fact that there were only a few hours left, she might expedite things by making a suggestion or two. Rand needed a little nudge. And if things moved as they should, Nadine's life would never be in jeopardy again.

The lower life form was once again admiring its portrait as she vanished from the room.

CHAPTER 40

At the red light at the intersection of Main and Chestnut, the teen sitting behind the wheel of the red MG convertible revved his engine.

An old woman with a cane stepped down carefully from the curb and limped across the street. She was almost directly in front of the sportscar when the light changed.

Rand leaned against the brick wall of the alley separating the bank from the Savings & Loan and sensed disaster. He stared directly at the MG and thought, *Stall*.

The little sportscar bucked as its driver jerked his leg, causing the clutch to release too abruptly.

The old woman reached the curb safely.

The impatient teen started the engine back up, flipped it into gear and squealed rubber as the car leaped forward.

"*What were you doing?*" A cloud dispersing behind him revealed Harriet's slender white form.

He was genuinely pleased to see her. Despite her irritating vanishing acts, he was growing quite fond of her. There was something warm and familiar about her. He was convinced that he'd known someone like her before. "*I don't like the way some people drive,*" he said. "*I was just making a few adjustments.*"

"*Someone who died the way you did should definitely have strong opinions about that. But what does it have to do with that boy?*"

"He might have given that old lady a coronary."

"What old lady?"

"The one trying to cross the street."

"You mean the one I can't see right now?"

He peered around the corner. No sign of her. *"She probably went into the bank right now. She'd be dead if I hadn't done something. And I didn't even have to be lady's-mannish, either."*

"I'm so pleased with your progress."

"Where did you go, by the way?"

"Later. We've got two quick stops to make. Niemus is up to his dirty tricks and we've got to head him off at the pass."

"This is beginning to sound like a bad western."

"Can't you forget about movie trivia for a second?"

"Not when you make a statement like that."

"Forgive me. I'm the old-fashioned type."

"Katherine Hepburn talking to Spencer Tracy. Desk Set, *nineteen-fifty-seven."*

She sighed. *"I asked for that one, didn't I?"*

"Try saying something that wasn't in a movie."

"Is that possible?"

"You might get lucky. Eventually."

"How about this? We're wasting valuable time standing here like idiots."

"That sounds like Mel Brooks."

"You're a mess, did you know that?"

"You've said that before."

"Only because I really mean it."

256

***

Betsy knew she should be tactful.

These days you couldn't determine a man's financial situation by his clothes. In this town, rich men wore bib overalls or tank tops and baggy shorts and walked around with their fly open half the time. She managed a smile and concentrated on her new customer's face, which was *very* easy on the eyes.

"May I help you?"

He returned her smile. "I'd like to speak with someone who handles the checking accounts."

"That would be Patti. Let's see if she's free now." She disappeared around the corner.

Betsy returned a minute later. "Patti's free," she said. "If you'll just turn to your right, she's the first office on your left down the hall."

"By the way, that's a lovely outfit you're wearing."

She'd bought it last week at the Mall but hadn't received any compliments yet. It sure looked good when she tried it on. It made her eyes large and brilliant.

"Why, *thank* you." She blushed like a teenager. With men you had to be careful because you never knew what they were thinking. But she saw only sincerity on his handsome, unshaven face.

"It brings out the golden quality in your eyes."

She was still blushing as he disappeared around the corner.

***

Abner Hargrove tried very hard to hide his contempt as he invited Monty into the office.

257

As president of the Barnes Savings & Loan *("people are our business, our collateral, & our pride!")*, Abner had been dealing with the public more than forty years, earning the reputation for helping people rather than taking advantage of them. It took substantial time and much effort to build up a solid trust. And even though Monty Niemus considered himself a legitimate businessman, Abner didn't share the same opinion. Monty took no prisoners when his X-ray vision zeroed in on a deal.

Elm Street was the present hot topic. The scuttlebutt was that this area could easily be converted into a condominium site. There was room for expansion, as well as a beautiful pine grove and other lush scenery surrounding it that would make the project a pleasant—and highly profitable—setting.

While this sort of thing had been the ongoing madness for the last few years, Abner wanted Barnes to stay as it was. He had no intention of contributing his resources to help make it another "Condo City."

He risked a quick glance at his watch. Could he possibly end this unpleasantness in five minutes? That was being unduly optimistic. But he'd do his level best to finish it as quickly as possible.

"How have you been, Monty?" Abner produced a cherry cigar box and flipped it open.

"Just lovely, thanks." Niemus carefully selected a slim ten-dollar imported cigar. He sniffed it, nodded his approval and tucked it away in his jacket pocket while lowering his sizeable butt into the chair.

Abner busied himself with his own cigar. Having been through this same routine with Niemus half a dozen times during the last few years, Abner knew what would transpire. But this bit of business would be especially distasteful. Abner was fond of Nadine. She was intelligent, pleasant to talk to, and incredibly pleasing to look at. If it hadn't been for Nadine's quick thinking, Abner's wife might have died after suffering her seizure in the Five'n Dime a couple of years ago. Nadine phoned it in immediately then stayed with Mabel, checking her airways and vitals, talking to her, and making sure she was comfortable. And when the medical unit arrived, she relayed the necessary information as efficiently as any trained professional.

Abner made himself a promise. If Niemus wanted Nadine's property, Abner would see to it that the transaction would be as difficult and as aggravating as humanly possible.

***

The nameplate on the office desk said Patti Holbrook.

Over forty and plump, she obviously spent much time and money on her frosted brown hair. It was piled high on her head like a beehive. She almost frowned at Rand's appearance but perked right up when he flashed a beaming smile in her direction.

"May I help you?"

"Yes. I'd like to discuss checking accounts with you."

"I don't believe I've ever seen you before, sir. New in town?"

"In a manner of speaking."

"May I ask your name?"

"Just call me Jerry."

She kept up the eye contact while awaiting additional information. When he didn't provide any she said, "Your last name?"

"Don't need one."

She picked up a ballpoint pen from her desk blotter and tapped it gently, her eyes dropping to his clothes— as if they would provide some sort of clue to this mystery.

A nut, maybe? she was probably thinking. *Could be, judging by the clothes.*

"I...don't quite understand," she said.

"Your hair," he said suddenly, smiling.

"P-Pardon me?"

He shrugged. "It's breathtaking."

Her face lit up. The ballpoint thumped quietly to the blotter. "Why, *thank* you." She reached up and patted it very gently, barely touching it for fear of altering the masterpiece.

"Would you mind if I did something?" Rand rose from his chair, reached across the desk, and lightly touched the woman's cheek. He sat back down. *"How's that, Harriet?"*

"Nauseating, but fine."

"She's ready now?"

"You can do whatever you like."

260

The woman's face had turned bright red. She wanted to exhibit an emotion but wasn't quite sure which one would be appropriate.

"W-Why did you do that, Mister, er…Jerry?"

"It's…your skin." He smiled sheepishly. "I wanted to find out for myself if it's as soft and as smooth as it looks."

"*Tacky, Rand.*"

"*The only thing I could think of at the moment.*"

"And *is* it?" Patti asked softly.

"Just as smooth as silk."

Blinking, she sat back in her chair.

"I hope I didn't embarrass you…"

"Oh, no! Of *course* you didn't."

"*You really need to be a little more subtle,*" Harriet said. "*At least, with your flirting.*"

"*But it's so much fun…*"

"*And you do it so well.*"

"*Thank you.*"

"*You know why I'm letting you do it now, don't you?*"

"*I'll bet you're about to tell me.*"

"*We're in a hurry, and it's the only thing that'll work so quickly. This woman obviously hasn't been with a man in a long time.*"

"*She's showing the signs. She probably wouldn't mind having me on a sandwich platter.*"

"*I don't think she'd need the bread. Or the platter.*"

Finally recovering, Patti Holbrook leaned forward and rested her elbows on her desk blotter.

261

The valley between her breasts, evident in the V-cut of her blue dress, deepened. She made no effort to hide it.

"*Now she's being just a tad obvious,*" Harriet said. "*I'm surprised she doesn't just put them on the table so you can see them better.*"

Patti cleared her throat and took a breath. "Just why did you come to see us, Jerry?"

"I'd like to discuss a certain checking account with you."

She blinked. "I'm sure you realize we're forbidden to discuss such personal information…"

"Yes. I know."

"*Toss her another smile.*"

Rand did as Harriet suggested.

"But in your case," Patti quickly added with a sly wink, "I think we can make a teensy-weensy exception…"

CHAPTER 41

Abner pushed a tendril of blue-gray cigar smoke toward the ceiling.

"Any particular reason why you're so determined to acquire this property?" he asked.

"I'm a businessman, Abner," Monty said in his usual smugness. "I've got definite plans for that area that would be of great benefit to this town."

"You realize, of course, it isn't ethical for me to discuss any particulars of the foreclosure until Nadine's extension is up. The woman still has one full day to come up with the money."

"Less than that, actually. Tomorrow starts the weekend. Monday's the scheduled day for the foreclosure. She only has an hour or two, if you want to get technical."

Abner didn't like this at all. Monty was enjoying himself entirely too much. "However little time she has, it's too early for us to be talking about this."

"I'll tell you this confidentially, Abner." Niemus' grin was more disturbing than usual. "There's no way Nadine will be able to come up with the amount due."

Abner placed his elbows on his desk blotter and tried very hard to refrain from asking Niemus to get out of his office. "And how would you know that?"

Niemus sighed and glanced at his manicured nails. "I've got my methods."

Abner frowned. "This is beginning to sound extremely unethical."

263

"It's nothing that should compromise you or this institution. No need to worry about it at all."

It was time to go at this more vigorously. Niemus being privy to the girl's financial situation made Abner want to grind his teeth.

"You understand, of course, that this bank is obligated to announce foreclosures publicly? In terms of legalities—"

"I'm aware of all that. I've done this same thing many times before."

"This institution has been operating nearly half a century. I'm not about to do anything that will compromise *any* aspect of our tradition of helping people. And what you are doing now is—"

"I'm simply informing you that your money will not be jeopardized," Monty said. "When an account goes in arrears, your primary option, of course, is—"

"Now you're attempting to tell me my business?"

"I'm just trying to touch base with you, making sure we're on the same level."

Abner wanted to tell the man that they could never be on the same level. But being a gentleman prevented him from reacting foolishly. "This foreclosure won't even be discussed until the end of this month. Which, I'm sure you know, is next week."

Niemus sat back and rubbed his jaw. Abner could practically hear the gears grinding inside the large head. "Anything wrong with my looking over the paperwork on the mortgage property itself?"

"The public documents? No. Anything else? Off-limits."

"I'm aware of that. We've done this before."

"And everything's always been legal. It's the only way I'll do business."

"Then I don't see a problem—do you?"

"The problem *I* see is that you've mentioned having inside knowledge of a mortgagee's accounts. As a result, I choose not to participate in any aspect of this matter."

"What's bugging you, Abner? I happen to know Nadine can't possibly come up with the money. The girl works at the Five'n Dime, for God's sake. Makes what? Nine-fifty, ten bucks an hour, tops?"

"I don't see what Nadine's wages have to do with this."

"It's a matter of protecting your investment, isn't it?"

"Protecting my investment would mean Nadine coming up with the money so she can keep her house."

"And if someone else takes it over and pays off the mortgage? As long as it's legal, why should it bother you?"

"Legally, it shouldn't. Morally and ethically? It bothers me infinitesimally."

"Your condo hang-up again?"

Abner took a breath. "I don't consider the idea of trying to keep this town as it is a *hang-up*."

Niemus sat back and shook his head. Abner wanted to pull it right off the man's shoulders and toss it in the trash. "Listen…I know you're old-fashioned. In fact, I respect that—to a degree. But where progress is concerned—"

"There are many flavors of progress."

"Progress is progress."

Abner was not about to let Niemus have the last word. "If I can get folks out of clapboard shacks and into newer, sounder dwellings I'll gladly do it because it improves the quality of life. If I can donate money to provide orphans with shoes and clothing, I'll do that, too. Other than those rare instances I embrace the outdated notion of keeping Barnes small and personable. And tearing down solid seventy-five-year-old houses to erect a block of multi-dwellings isn't going to—"

"This town is growing. People need somewhere to live."

Abner picked up his cigar and studied it. He knew he'd just run out of gas. Niemus was obviously prepared for anything. "I guess it won't hurt to have you look at the papers briefly before you leave." Abner jabbed a button on his box.

A female voice said, "Yes, Mister Hargrove?"

"The public documents for the Connelly property, eight-twenty-five Elm. Bring them in, Katherine."

"One moment."

Abner switched off. "I don't have many options during a foreclosure." It was difficult keeping the contempt out of his voice. "As I already told you, Nadine still has time to come up with the money."

"I understand completely."

"And despite what everyone thinks, we don't relish foreclosures. They're unpleasant, heartbreaking, and cause problems for all concerned."

"Yes. I know."

A knock at the door. Abner sighed. "Come in."

The door opened slowly.

Katherine, her face pale, stood stiffly in the hallway. She held open a slender brown folder and was studying it—as though she didn't believe what she was looking at.

Abner lifted a silver brow. "What's wrong?"

Katharine didn't speak. She was still studying the folder.

"Katharine? What is it?"

"This mortgage. It's been…paid *off*…"

Niemus jumped up. "By who?"

"Nadine Connelly…"

CHAPTER 42

The Savings & Loan was nearly empty when Rand and Harriet slipped through the revolving doors.

Behind the cage, a petite brunette in a white blouse and maroon skirt smiled at him. Her name plate said *Suzanne*.

"May I help you?"

"Ask her for a withdrawal slip," Harriet said.

"Is that all you want me to do?"

"Go ahead, knock yourself out. But do it quickly. This really nauseates me."

"You have a really beautiful smile."

"Thank you," she said, blushing.

"Do I need to touch her?"

"She's already melting." Harriet sighed. *"These females...I'm beginning to really worry about them."*

***

Harriet was silent when they went back outside.

At the street corner she watched the passing traffic. Something definitely was on her mind; he could tell by the way her head was tilted.

"What's wrong?" he asked.

"We need to be with Nadine."

"She's probably at work."

"She needs to stay home. At least for the next hour or so."

"Why?"

"I think it would be nice if you spent just a little more time with her."

"Any specific reason?"

"Just being careful." She raised a robe-covered arm.

Rand caught a glimpse of Nadine's wide-eyed husband staring directly at him one block away just before Harriet's warm cloud enveloped them both.

***

After two strong vodka martinis to settle his nerves, Ralph Connelly left the Barnes Café.

He felt a little better, but he still couldn't figure out what had happened at the bank. He'd always prided himself in his meticulousness. There was no logical way he could have misspelled Nadie's name as well as his own.

The two names splashed across his vision like one of those ads from a plane.

N-A-D-E-E-N C-O-N-L-I-E?

Hell, a first grader could have done a better job.

Even a moron knew how to spell his wife's name…

They'd pulled something at the bank—he was certain of it.

But how? And why?

He had to go back and talk to that teller's supervisor. There was no way he could've done such a silly thing. They needed to know he was much better than that. His reputation was at stake.

But what if they called Nadie to verify the mistake?

He'd deal with that later. Right now, he was going back to that bank and—

The sight halfway down the block made him cringe. What the *hell*?

He rubbed his eyes.

What was going on? Was that real or what?

He prided himself in his perfect 20-20 vision. But what he'd just glimpsed was something unbelievable. It looked like the bum he'd met the day before. The bum spending time with Nadie.

The bum Monty had paid the two rough customers five hundred big ones to beat up.

He'd just come out of the Savings & Loan building, took a couple of steps toward the curb, and vanished.

Impossible.

Unlikely, too, since there wasn't a mark anywhere on the man's face.

His imagination, most likely. He was still unnerved by that stupid check incident and wasn't thinking clearly.

Don't forget the martinis.

Of course. They made them strong at the Café. But...would just two of them cause him to see things?

One sure way to find out.

He ran down the street. Maybe the bum had seen Ralph and panicked.

That was what happened. He spotted Ralph and split. All Ralph had to do was track him down and let Monty know what was going on.

Ralph reached the alley entrance.

No sign of anyone.

***

Nadine, in gray sweatshirt and jeans, came from the kitchen carrying a mug of coffee.

Her hair, freshly washed, gleamed in the afternoon sunlight filtering through the living room curtains. It slid freely across her shoulders as she moved. She appeared healthier and more alert than the day before. When she saw Rand she nearly spilled the coffee.

"Did I forget to lock the door?" She glanced past him, at the front entrance.

"You'd better be more careful," he said. "Too many creeps roaming around these days."

"Lots on my mind, I guess."

The dreamy quality in her eyes made Rand uncomfortable. Luckily Harriet was standing close.

"I'm glad you came back," Nadine said. "We need to talk some more."

"About what? My grandfather?"

"No. You."

Rand swallowed.

"There's something about you, Jerry. Something I can't quite pin down."

"Maybe it's my impeccable taste in clothing," he said uneasily.

She set the coffee mug on the mantelpiece. "I think it's a little more than that."

"My wry wit? Dashing good looks?"

"Why don't we talk about it?"

"What about work?"

"I called in sick again."

"You're still not feeling well?"

"Actually, I feel just fine."

"Then why—"

"Let's go for a walk, okay?"

"*Harriet*?"

She'd vanished.

CHAPTER 43

The check was made out for fifty thousand dollars.

Where in God's creation did Nadine get her claws on that much money?

Abner Hargrove held the cashier's check carefully in both hands. He looked like he was really enjoying this, the pompous jerk.

"When did this come in, Katherine?" Hargrove asked.

"I don't know, I must not have been in the office at the time."

This made no sense. None whatsoever. Nadine was in no financial position to have stumbled onto that much cash. Even if she had, wouldn't she have mentioned it?

"The check *cleared?*" Monty wanted to rip the damned thing out of Hargrove's hands and have the signature X-rayed.

"Y-Yes, sir." Katherine was avoiding Monty's glare. "It's stamped on the back of the check. It cleared yesterday."

"Nadine barely makes thirty grand a year. How could she possibly manage such a huge payoff?"

The corners of his mouth lifting slightly, Hargrove said, "I hear she works a lot of overtime."

"Don't be funny." Monty waited patiently for the surge of heat to pass. "This is serious."

"She might have come into an inheritance recently. Don't rule that out. She could have relatives we don't know about."

Monty had done considerable research when the subject of the foreclosure first reached his desk. The entire Grove family fortune, at the time of both parents' deaths, amounted to the house which, when the mortgage was paid off, was sold, the tiny profits divided equally amongst the three daughters. Other than a nine-year-old Ford van and less than three grand in furnishings, there was nothing.

"What's the date on the check?" he asked.

Hargrove turned it over. "Two days ago."

Monty's scalp buzzed.. Nadine had written it the same day they met at the Café. The same day she was terrified that her husband was making arrangements behind her back to sell the house.

Something wasn't right.

"I can't remember anyone mentioning such a huge deposit," Hargrove said to Katherine. "Are you sure you don't remember Nadine coming in?"

"No, sir. This is a complete surprise."

"What's *that* tell you, Abner?"

"It could've slipped the cashier's mind. We handle so many accounts..."

"You don't personally recall her coming in just two days ago and paying off her house?"

Hargrove shrugged. "Like I said, we've got entirely too many customers to keep track of. And I'm not always in the office. I enjoy lunch at the country club most afternoons and usually get back somewhat late." He smiled sheepishly. "Sorry, Monty, but some of us need to escape work now and then."

CHAPTER 44

It was a beautiful afternoon.

Leaves slid from a metal roof, dropping silently to the grass. A gust of cool air swept through the pines peppering the valley.

Harriet had vanished again, but it didn't bother him this time. Rand suspected she wanted them to have some privacy.

Nadine hadn't said anything since they stepped outside. She moved easily, her arms crossed in front of her. He could tell she was thinking of what had happened earlier, in her bathroom.

"You're so quiet," he said. "Anything wrong?"

Her eyes were as bright as the sun glinting through the fluffy clouds in the sky. "Everything's wonderful." But it sounded almost like a question.

"You seem skeptical."

A shrug. "There's no logical reason for things to be this way."

She was indeed very perceptive. It was important to get her to accept the situation.

"Why not enjoy it while it lasts?" he asked.

"Just a short while ago I'd hit rock bottom. I found out about my illness, then received the foreclosure notice. It was the worst time of my life—far worse than when my mother or father died, or when I was given the task of dividing their will equally among my sisters. And when I started having trouble with Monty and Ralph, I didn't want to go through much more." She stopped walking. "But when I met you, all the bad stuff just…stopped…"

He avoided her eyes.

"It *was* because of you, wasn't it?"

"All I did was get Niemus off your back." His heart was pounding so much that he thought she might be able to hear it above the passing traffic.

She moved closer. He could feel himself crumbling as Nadine's eyes bored into him. "Tell me who you are, Jerry. Who you *really* are."

He shrugged. "The grandson of—"

"Besides that."

"A guy who didn't like the raw deal you were getting."

"But how'd you even know about me? About my problems? I never saw you before."

He wanted to interfere with her thoughts, add some blankness to confuse her, stop the questions…but each time he tried, the hopeful look on her face stopped him.

"You can't possibly know *everyone* in town, can you?" he asked.

"I work at the Five'n Dime. You said that yourself. Everyone goes there."

His pulse quickened even more.

"Tell me how you knew, Jerry. How you showed up at the perfect moment. You still haven't said why you showed up or how you got me to open up to   you. And I don't mean just minor things. You're the only person I've ever talked to about Rand Powell. I've been keeping him bottled up inside me for fifteen years."

He could feel his composure collapsing steadily.

"*Please* tell me what's going on…"

278

CHAPTER 45

Monty Niemus stepped outside and took several gulps of fresh air. When the heat of anger and the dizziness finally subsided, he began to think more clearly.

Didn't make any sense. Not at all. There was no way in hell Nadine could come up with fifty thousand dollars for a mortgage payoff. It just wasn't possible.

"Mr. Niemus?"

Monty spun around.

Connelly was standing just a few feet away. His face was paler than usual; he was out of breath.

This wasn't the time for surprises. "Where the hell did *you* come from? I didn't even—"

"Something strange is going on."

"What's wrong with you? You look like something just scared the living snot out of you. But you're certainly right about strange crap. You'll never guess what your wife just did."

"Mr. Niemus…that man you paid those two drunks to beat up…"

Monty could only hear one thing in his head. It was the only thing that existed right now. The only thing he couldn't understand. The only thing that really mattered. "She paid off the house…"

"What was that?"

"Your impoverished wife somehow came up with the fifty thousand she needed to pay off the damned house. How the hell did she do that? Tell me where she found the money."

Connelly's eyes bulged. "There's…no way she could have done that."

"You have no idea either?"

"I drained whatever she did have—which wasn't much. But fifty thousand? She suddenly found fifty thousand dollars?"

"Not suddenly. Two days ago."

"That makes no sense."

"A lot of things haven't made any sense lately. I'm beginning to wonder about that bum who's been sticking his nose—"

"That's what I wanted to tell you, Mr. Niemus. I just saw him."

"He's out of the hospital already?"

"There wasn't a mark on him."

Monty's face flushed. "You're kidding me..."

"Not a mark—I swear."

"Dammit. Those two drunken assholes took my five bills and ran. Where'd you see this guy?"

"He ducked in the alley next to the Savings & Loan when he saw me."

"So you don't know where he went."

"He got away fast."

Monty rubbed his temples. He was getting the feeling that the bum they were after wasn't a bum. It still baffled him that the man knew what brand of outfit Monty was wearing yesterday and the day before. How the hell could a bum know *that*?

But if he wasn't a bum, who was he? And why was he dressed like a bum?

One thing was for certain: ever since he'd come into the picture, things hadn't happened as they should have.

"What do we do, Mr. Niemus? He could be anywhere."

"He's probably back with Nadine."

"You think so?"

"Where else would he be? He's been sticking close to her ever since I first saw him."

"I guess that makes sense."

"Of course it does. I also know what has to be done. We've got to find out who this joker really is, and that's going to take serious cash."

"I'm beginning to think he really isn't a bum."

"I've known a few bums in my time, Connelly. They don't act like this guy."

"I think you're right. A bum would've asked her for money or stolen a few things from the house. And I really don't think Nadie would let a genuine panhandler con his way into her house."

"I think I'd better pay the bank a visit. I know exactly who we need to employ this time."

Connelly swallowed. "Don't tell me you're gonna pay someone else—"

"There's a private detective in St. Clairsville I've used before. He charges five hundred a day. His retainer is five thousand."

"That's a lot of money."

"I think that when a project worth nine figures is at stake, five thousand's a really cheap price for finding out who we're dealing with here."

CHAPTER 46

Rand forced himself to look away from the beautiful pleading eyes.

Just as he did, a flash went off in his head—a toddler being struck down by a pickup truck in the middle of the street.

He spun around. Straight ahead, the toddler was running out into the street after a large white rubber ball rolling down the sloped drive.

A moment later, the roar of the pickup squealed around the corner, past the Burger King. It was heading right for the child.

"Oh my *God...*" Nadine covered her mouth.

Rand's thoughts were quick and to the point: *alley-oop, little guy.*

Just as the truck swerved, some invisible force yanked the toddler by his shirt collar and pulled gently, until he was sitting on the sidewalk.

The truck screeched to a stop a couple of houses down.

A man and a woman ran down the driveway. The woman was crying in hysterics. The man scooped up the child and yelled at the truck driver, who was getting out to see if the child was all right.

Realizing what he had just done, Rand turned around.

Nadine was gazing wide-eyed at him.

***

Nadine's mind instantly clicked into rewind.

Recalling details, she fought to put together some semblance of logic. But what she saw—or *thought* she saw—didn't make sense.

Her eyes playing tricks?

Or was it stress? Continued exposure to trauma often leads to mental and physical symptoms such as anxiety and depression, dyspepsia, palpitations, muscular aches and pains, and other assorted ailments.

Such as what? Delusions?

Was that another symptom? She couldn't remember. Too much stress, apparently, to be able to think clearly.

All right. Thinking clearly was a chore right now. But was she seeing things?

What she'd seen was as real as the pavement under her feet. Jerry spinning around, his whole body tensing. The child being picked up and pulled out of the way by some invisible force. Afterward, Jerry relaxing.

Dizziness beckoned; she closed her eyes and waited.

For what?

Why, for logic to explain what she'd actually seen. To tell her that what she thought she'd just seen did not happen.

Why did she think Jerry had done that? Why was she certain he had?

Do you believe in magic?

Relax. Let the coolness of the day caress your skin, the afternoon sun warm your cheeks. Tell yourself nothing's bothering you. Soon you'll be home again, where you can relax on the couch and finish that cup of coffee.

She forced her eyes open. And when she did, she could have sworn Jerry had changed, had somehow turned into Rand. And when he turned to look at her, he wore the same expression she'd seen on the overpass—

It *wasn't* a dream after all.

My God... Jerry...isn't...real...

She didn't know how she knew; she just knew nothing else made any sense of any of this.

The events of the last two days thundered into her consciousness.

Dreams that weren't really dreams.

A stranger coming into her life almost like a puff of smoke.

Her wrinkles disappearing.

Now, after months of sadness and despair, she'd felt an almost heavenly presence...

It was as if Rand Powell had actually come back and—

Her balled fist shot up to her mouth.

Oh my dear God...

CHAPTER 47

Avoiding the searing gaze of her customer, Alice carefully double-checked her figures.

This was not going to be pleasant. When you looked after other folks' money you were already in dangerous waters. But when you were involved with important money, such the large account of the man standing stiffly on the other side of her cage, you were in *deep*.

Monty Niemus was responsible for the playground the city had built down the street from her house, where Marie and Kenny, her two kids, spent so many afternoons after school. Monty Niemus was someone you didn't want to mess with. He was one of the most important men in town. More important, he had a hair-trigger temper and had been known to go ballistic on many an occasion.

He finally said, "Problem?"

What Alice had just found out was so terrible, she wanted to vanish into thin air and reappear in a different place. This was serious. Like it or not, it had fallen into her lap. Niemus had to know.

But she just couldn't find the right words.

His glare deepened, telling her that hair-trigger temper was about to be put into immediate action.

Her heart was in her mouth when she said, "It's…well, sir, your account…"

"What about my account?"

The door was only twenty feet away. She could get out of there in a couple of seconds if she was lucky. All she had to do was turn and rush down the aisle. Then she could cut down the hall and make her escape out the rear entrance. Her VW was parked only about twenty feet from the rear door. It wouldn't take her more than thirty seconds to get in the car and hightail it out of there.

But where would she go? What would she do? She couldn't very well just leave the bank and—

"Tell me the problem!"

Her whole body had become cold and weak. After a deep breath she stammered out, "There's not enough money…to cover…this withdrawal."

***

Not enough money?

Monty grabbed the counter for balance. Connelly was standing directly behind him. Monty wanted him gone. He didn't want anyone to see him lose it. But as his blood pressure rose steadily, he thought it might be a good thing Connelly was standing by.

He tried reading the bank teller's face, but she'd lowered it. All he could see was a giant clump of heavily sprayed red hair with some gray roots peeking through the center like thin wire coils. Maybe he hadn't heard her right. Maybe she was trying to say something else.

"Let me get this straight. You can't give me five thousand dollars because there's not enough money in my account to cover it?"

A slight nod.

There was absolutely no logic to this nonsense. He was a millionaire. His assets alone were rapidly

286

approaching eight figures. His real estate holdings were enough to put him on Easy Street for the remainder of his life. Not to mention his antiques, vehicles, jewelry, and coin collection. His stocks and bonds were worth a fortune. His ready cash—the smallest portion of his worth—amounted to a sum which would enable him to purchase any large chunk of top-level commercial real estate in the Ohio Valley.

He rested his elbows on the counter. It was a difficult moment, but he managed to refrain from reaching through the bars and grabbing the stupid twit's neck.

"I maintain checking and savings accounts in every bank in this town." He struggled to keep his voice soft and steady. "I have three separate accounts in this bank alone. I carry a checking account and two separate savings accounts with this establishment. Just a few hours ago I had more than ten thousand dollars in checking, twenty-five thousand in a Primary Share account, and fifteen thousand in a Money Market account. That adds to up more than fifty thousand—"

My God...

Fifty thousand dollars.

The figure splashed brightly in his head like a starburst. Something eerily familiar about it made his limbs shudder. Something about that amount—

"Mr. Niemus?" Connelly was behind him, tapping his forearm.

The mortgage.

Things not making sense.

The room grew warm, began to spin. The redhead faded into a liquid haze.

His voice was a raspy croak. "Bring me the bank manager!"

CHAPTER 48

"Who *are* you, Jerry?" Nadine asked, her face pale. "I mean really."

Oh boy... Rand knew then that he'd better be very careful.

"You must be awfully special." Nadine's eyes still filled the sockets. "To do what you did? That really was something."

"It was nothing."

Her eyes grew. "You pick up a little boy from a hundred feet away and say it's *nothing*?"

"How do you know I did that?"

"I know, Jerry. I know you did it."

"How can you be so sure?"

"I don't know. I just know you did it."

"There's no way I can convince you that—"

"Tell me the truth." Her hands were balled into tight white fists at her sides.

"Would you believe me if I said I've always been good at mind-over-matter stuff?"

"No..."

"How about beginner's luck?"

She was beginning to get angry. "You're playing with me. I'd like to know why. I thought we were friends."

"We are."

"Then tell me what you did. How you saved that little boy's life."

"Listen, Nadine—"

"You know you did, so stop playing."

"Playing is what I do when I don't know what else to do."

"Tell me, Jerry."

He sighed and rubbed the back of his neck. "I…don't know where to begin."

"For openers you can tell me how long you've been in town."

Rand could feel his sanity slipping steadily. "I've…been here a couple of days."

"*Three* days, maybe?"

A shiver climbed up his spine.

On the overpass she'd called out his name. She'd seen him. He was wearing a different covering, but she'd somehow penetrated it. Maybe she *had* been thinking of him at the time. But that had nothing to do with now, did it?

"That's about right," he told her.

"You never did tell me where you're from. If you lived here when your grandfather was alive."

His eyes ached for a glimpse of the slender white figure. Harriet would help him out. She'd tell him what to say so Nadine wouldn't know she was actually talking to the man she'd loved half her life, a man who was now dead.

"And you're not going to, are you?" she asked in his silence.

"I can't…"

She moved closer. Her large probing eyes made him turn away. He suspected she'd just searched his soul and found a few pieces of the puzzle already. "You're not real, Jerry." It was whispered logically—as if she'd just told him he needed a shave. "When you first saw me, you mentioned magic. I should have suspected something then, but I didn't. I wanted so much for something magical to happen that I didn't care about anything else. And I was so...so surprised by how you snuck up on me." She paused. He could tell she was searching again, looking for something else. "You *didn't* sneak up on me, did you?"

"*Harriet?*"

"You *appeared*." When he didn't respond she said, "*Please* tell me the truth. I have to know."

His mind worked feverishly. The harder he agonized, the bleaker everything became. He was Rand Powell. He *couldn't* lie—doing so had always been against his code of ethics. It wasn't the right thing to do, and led to more lies. But telling Nadine the truth would be disastrous. Yet he *wanted* her to know who he really was. He needed her to know.

And he wanted her to know how he felt, how she'd affected his life.

"You know, the more I look at you, the more you remind me of him." A quiet azure glow emanated from her.

"That was a long time ago," he said.

"It's stayed with me all these years."

"It was a crush—"

"It *wasn't* a crush," she said in a soft voice. She was suddenly far away. The glow, now a soft sheen of flowing satin, surrounded her. She was watching the pine trees across the street. There was a distant look in her eye. She'd gone back again to a time when she was young and happy, and love was a mysterious exciting thing that awakened her senses, showing her what it meant to be a woman. "It was true love."

***

Rand always thought Nadine had gone through something all young girls experience when their hormones are developing.

But now he realized that whatever she'd endured was much more than a schoolgirl's crush. She was now a grown woman who'd been carrying around his memory for years—which told him that what had happened to him had also happened to her.

He struggled within his soul for the right thing to say. To get at the truth, however bizarre.

But instead, whatever logic he was searching for had been eclipsed by something much more important. He'd gone back, this time to recall, once and for all, how it ended.

CHAPTER 49

Rand's new profession in software sales was coming along slowly.

Over the summer months he'd gained valuable contacts in Wheeling, Pittsburgh, and also in Tampa and Orlando, where software had been booming the last few years.

But after three months of becoming more and more obsessed with Nadine, Rand realized that moving away might be the most sensible solution. His profession required concentration, not distraction. In Wheeling he'd be in a much better position to immerse himself in his work.

He believed the idea was sound. The more he thought of it, the more he realized there might not be another option. Wheeling was just far enough away where the move wouldn't disrupt his schedule. In six months, he'd be in great shape.

But he couldn't get past the idea of living half an hour away from Nadine without being able to see her. He knew he'd come back in the evenings or on weekends to see if he could spot her on the street—or in the Burger King, watching for him.

Rand left the house one evening to take in the cool night air. He'd hoped he might arrive at a reasonable solution in this more relaxed setting.

But just two blocks from his house, he heard the shuffle of soft footsteps behind him. Nadine, in tank top, cutoff jeans and tennis shoes, had been following him. Her hair hung loose, making her look older, more mature.

Rand stopped cold, turned, and numbly watched her continue to approach him.

The silence was heavy and awkward as they stared at one another. Rand wanted to say something clever to lighten the moment, but all he could do was gape numbly at her and listen to the heavy thumping of his own heart.

He knew she wanted him to say something. After all, he was staring directly at her, wasn't he? He couldn't just stand there like that and say nothing. He was older and wiser. More mature. A success-minded young man in today's world. He was about to embark on a new career in software—he'd be meeting people, making contacts. The gift of gab should always be there, ready to be unleashed.

But as much as he wanted to take control of the situation, the silence continued. His brain had wandered off to explore other lands. The way she was watching him only made him self-conscious. He was wearing frayed jeans and an oversized sweatshirt but glanced down at himself anyway to make sure every wrinkle, every fold, was perfect.

Nadine wasn't looking at his ensemble; she was studying his face. "I've wanted to thank you for a long time," she said, her voice as soft as the breeze.

"For what?"

"For saving my life."

"It was my pleasure."

She smiled and looked down. He could tell she was blushing even though the darkness clouded her face. "I also wanted to tell you that I'm glad it happened."

He couldn't reply. He knew it wouldn't be very bright to tell her that he was thinking the very same thing.

"I...felt safe...in your arms. I've felt that way...ever since."

"You've...got a crush on me, don't you?" He didn't know why he'd said it. But he somehow felt obligated to tell her he knew.

She shook her head. "Not a crush."

"You...don't even know me."

"Does it matter?"

She'd somehow transformed into a woman rapidly approaching the time in her life when being in love was very important. He couldn't possibly know how she really felt about him—he only knew how he felt about her. The smart thing would be to tell her and hope she'd understand.

"Yes, it matters," he said.

"Why?"

"You're too young."

"I may be young and naive and silly...but I know my heart." Tears welled in her eyes. "I want you to know something else. I wish—"

Rand pressed a finger gently to her lips. They were soft and warm, stirring something inside him. The forbidden thoughts came back, but instead of forcing them away, as he'd done frequently during

295

the last few months, he decided they should be carefully stored in a special place.

"I want you to know something, too."

It was important to choose his words carefully. He was about to say something that was going to hurt. But maybe it wouldn't if he said it the right way.

"I want you to know that no matter how you feel, nothing can ever come of this. And even though I might feel the same—"

"*Do* you?" Her wet eyes grew. "Do you *really*?"

He had to be especially careful now. He was touching her heart, and it was very fragile.

"I can only say that if I did, it would be a waste. Because of who you are and who I am. It would be a mistake to admit to anything."

"Even though it feels so right?"

He shushed her again. The warm tear dropping onto his knuckle made him tremble.

"You have to forget about this crush—"

"*Not* a crush."

"—So you can grow up to become the woman you're destined to be."

He could tell she wanted to speak, but no words left her parted lips.

"What would you like to be?" he asked. "Don't you want to go to college or something?"

"I'd like to study medicine. They say I have an aptitude for it."

"That sounds great. Where would you like to study?"

"California. Stanford has a great heart disease program. Then there's Keck at USC. Geffen also has a terrific school at UCLA. Both Stanford and Keck sent me their literature. They said my grades are good enough

for a partial scholarship."

"You ought to give it all you've got. You know what you want, so—"

"I thought I did…"

"What's changed?"

She looked down at her feet, then back up at him. Her eyes glinted in the darkness. "Everything changed when I saw you. Now I'm not sure about anything anymore."

"You have to go after your dreams." It hurt him to say this, to pull himself out of her world, but he knew he had to. It was the right thing to do, and it was the truth. He couldn't let her give up at such a young age. "You owe it to yourself. This is your one crack at life. Start thinking of yourself. Forget about me. We can never be together."

"Don't you even…*like* me?"

"Very much." The words were heavy and warm in his throat.

She smiled, but only for a moment. Her smile quickly faded, turning into sadness. "If two people love one another but don't do anything about it…isn't that wrong?"

She'd touched him deeply and it hurt. It hurt so much that he feared he might fall apart if he didn't soon leave.

His mind deserted him again, and he turned away.

"Please, Rand. Don't leave…"

Her cheeks were wet. He wanted to wipe the tears away. He wanted to wipe away anything that made her unhappy.

"Grow up, Nadine. Give life a chance. One day you'll meet someone who'll make you forget about me."

"Never!"

His heart bursting, he tried once again to walk away. "*Please* don't walk away from me…"

He stopped. He had to think of something bright and sensible. He was the adult and should be in full control of his actions.

But when he turned around, he found that she'd snuck up to him. Her face was only inches away.

They kissed, and he knew he was deeply in love.

He put his hands on her tiny shoulders and flinched at their warmth, the trembling in them. It startled him, made him pull away.

But the fact that he'd done it so slowly, so reluctantly, scared him. In fact, he knew deep down that he hadn't wanted to stop the kiss at all.

This brought him to his senses.

He knew at that moment that he could no longer stay in this town. He also knew he couldn't move a mere thirty miles away. It would be much too close.

"No. We…can't do this."

"Rand…"

His heart bursting, he hurried away. She called his name.

He knew that if he stopped even for a moment, he'd go back to her. He could no longer trust his feelings.

That same night he packed his bags.

Early the next morning, he drove to Orlando, Florida.

CHAPTER 50

"It was true love," Nadine said in a soft voice.

Rand's composure was on the verge of collapse.

"Rand told me how he felt that day," she went on. "He said he liked

me but I had the feeling it was more than that. But then he moved away and I never saw him again. It was so *sudden*… I was *so* hurt, I moped around for weeks. I'd often wondered why he'd gone. If it was because of me." She smiled faintly. "I guess it was the romantic in me. But then I remembered what Clancy told me about Rand's home business. I figured Rand had to relocate. So for the next few months I tried forgetting about him. For a while I thought I had…but I guess I was just deceiving myself. He never *really* left me, you know? From then on, whenever I was with any other guy, I compared him to Rand."

"How about your husband?"

"I met Ralph right after I'd started my career in medicine. My mind was on so much other stuff that my Rand fantasy was shoved aside. But not long after my honeymoon, I started thinking about him again. That probably makes me sound cold-hearted, but that's just the way it was."

He wanted to tell her what happened but didn't want to say anything that would hurt her.

"Do *you* know, Jerry?" She searched his eyes. "Do *you* have any idea why he moved away so quickly? Your grandfather might have known something. Did he say anything? I mean, did he mention Rand moving away?"

"Rand." Harriet appeared above a bush in someone's front yard.

"Where the hell were you?"

"Watching the fireworks in town."

"Jerry, please look at me..."

He turned—

The kiss was quick and hot. Despite his fears, his initial resistance, he closed his eyes and let it happen. He felt her trembling the way she had the first time. When the kiss ended, he stepped back. The stark look of recognition in her eyes caused a sheen of cold sweat to cover his borrowed face, and he shivered.

"R-Rand?"

A heavy wave of nausea thrashed through him.

"Oh, good..." Harriet covered her face.

"What the hell just happened?" He couldn't take his eyes off Nadine.

"Silly boy. Don't you know a woman always remembers a man's kiss? Especially if it was a real scorcher?"

"You're...*him*..." Nadine's eyes grew. "You don't *look* like him, but somehow...you're him. I don't know how, but you are. You're...*Rand*."

"Listen, Nadine—"

"We have to go." Harriet was tapping her left wrist, where a wristwatch would have been if she were alive. *"Now's a really nifty time, actually."*

"In the middle of all this?"

301

"We're finished. And since we've done everything we set out to do, it no longer matters what you tell her."

"I have no idea what to say."

"Tell her what's in your heart."

Truth. It was what Nadine wanted all along.

He placed his hands on her shoulders. Once again he had to be gentle, to say it just the right way. It would devastate her if he wasn't careful. But he realized that no matter how he said it, it was going to hurt.

"Nadine…Rand's no longer with us."

"No!" She brought up her hands to her mouth. "You're *him*. You've come *back*."

"I was. Once."

"You're…an *angel*?"

"I'm learning the ropes. Haven't earned my wings yet—as Clarence Oddbody would say."

"Will you please *stop the movie trivia?"* Harriet was shaking her head.

Her glistening eyes grew but stayed on him. "When…did it happen?" she asked in a little girl's voice.

"Not long ago. A car accident."

"My God…Did you…suffer?"

"It was a little uncomfortable, but what the hey, how much fun can you have when some idiot turns your ride into a pretzel with you in it?"

Her eyes dropped to his clothing. "How are you able to—"

302

"This ride's on loan." He forced a smile. "One of those short-term deals. Reasonable rates, with no penalties if I return it in its original condition."

"Cute," Harriet said.

"You're…really *him*?"

He nodded.

Nadine wiped away a tear. "Why did you move away…so quickly?"

"I'd fallen in love with you."

Her smile lit up her face.

"Why didn't you ever go to California?"

She lowered her face. "I…couldn't."

He cupped her chin in his hand and gently raised her head so she could look at him. "Why not?"

"I've…been waiting."

"Waiting?"

"For you to come back. I didn't want to be gone if…when you did."

"Nadine—"

"I knew you would. I just knew you would."

"Even if I had come back before, nothing could've happened. Wasn't in the cards, I guess."

"Things never happen the way they're supposed to. Life sucks, doesn't it?"

"Sometimes."

Nadine grew silent. When she spoke again, what came out tugged at his heart. "We would've been so *good* together."

"Wasn't in the Plan."

"What plan?"

"Life. Order. There's a definite plan. A reason for everything."

It was obvious by her dark look that she hadn't cared much for that. But she accepted it in silence.

Standing before him wasn't a grown woman whose heart was melting. She'd somehow turned back into the same skinny little girl who ran past his front porch so many times during the most difficult and wonderful summer of his life.

"One day there'll be another Rand," he said softly. "His name will be different, and he'll look different, but he'll make you forget all about me."

"You told me that before." She glared at him through wet eyes. "You know what I have to say about that, don't you?"

"Give him a chance, Nadine. You're special. You deserve the best."

"How will I know…it's him?"

"You'll see it in his eyes. They'll be just like Rand's eyes."

"*You know how much this movie trivia is getting to me, don't you?*" Harriet said sourly.

"*It seems to apply here.*"

"Will I…ever see you again?"

"One day, in another life."

"Maybe we can be together then."

"I'll keep that day open on my calendar."

"How can I thank you…for helping me?"

"By giving life another chance."

"*C'mon, Rand. We're burning daylight.*"

"*That's right out of a John Wayne flick.*"

Harriet sighed. *"I knew I shouldn't have opened my big mouth."*

"Will I be okay?" she asked. "I feel differently about things, but—"

"You'll be just fine. Promise me you'll go back to medicine. You'll be great at it."

"You really think so?"

"I'd go to you. And I hate doctors."

"Kiss her, Rand."

"What?"

"You heard me."

"Kiss her where?"

"You scum puppy. On the cheek. Go on. Just don't make a mess of it."

He moved toward Nadine. She quickly turned her head and their lips met again. She closed her eyes. When she tried wrapping her arms around his neck, nothing was there. He'd already begun fading.

"Rand?"

"Gotta go."

"Please stay."

"Sorry. I can't." A hazy white mist appeared.

"Just a few more minutes?"

"So long, Nadine. We'll see one another again. I promise."

"I'll *always* love you."

Warm ashen swirls encircled them. He had the sensation of rising.

"True love," her voice called. Rising, rising . . .

"Forever!"

EPILOGUE

Flickering white forms swirled around them.

"Why did you want me to kiss her?" Rand asked.

Harriet smiled. "To heal her."

"You mean my kiss made her well again?"

"Exactly."

"Wow. I've been told I was a good kisser, but—"

"Don't get carried away, Romeo. It has nothing to do with your puckering power."

"Why didn't you let me do that earlier? Wouldn't it have saved us time? And in my case, a lot of unnecessary angst?"

"She needed to be in a pure, advanced state of healing. It actually happened this morning, when she looked in the mirror. The process usually starts with appearance before graduating to attitude and inner strength. With the strength comes confidence and a sense of triumph. Soon there's no longer a need for depression or failure. Or heavenly guidance."

"So why was I so important in this?"

"When you left Barnes, you broke her heart. You were the one who actually started her decline."

Rand sighed. He'd never felt lower than at this moment.

"Don't beat yourself up, it happens. Anyway, she gradually mended. It took years, of course, but since she really wasn't in a hurry to get well in the first place, her heart remained fragile, and vulnerable enough to let in her sickness. But now, thanks to you, she's fully recovered, and she'll finally be able to see that it really was an illusion. Then she'll move on with her life."

"You think it was an illusion?"

"We all have them, don't we? I had one when I was mortal."

"Tell me about it."

"It was just one of those silly things resulting from a lost love."

"I'm sorry."

"I got over it."

Clouds twisted at their feet. Strong smells of orange blossoms, cinnamon, peppermint, and honeysuckle permeated the air. The sun gleamed a bright gold. Spatterings of every conceivable color and texture danced around it. Rooftops flicked by beneath them, visible an instant before feathery strands of clouds covered them. A distant rainbow splashed fireworks of deep color into the blue expanse of space.

"What if Niemus puts it together that I was the one who messed up his checking account?"

"He won't remember you."

At first he thought she was joking. But was she? Her expression was deadly serious. "Really?"

"He won't be able to. None of them will."

It registered coldly.

"None of them?"

"When an angel's work is finished, no mortal has the slightest recollection of what happened."

Rand felt a catch in his throat.

307

Harriet laughed. "Don't be so sensitive. You healed her, saved her life, let it begin afresh. That's no minor accomplishment."

"It's just hard to imagine that she won't remember the last three days. They certainly were rough for me."

"You'll always be with her. Now more than ever. She'll go through many more changes. A big chunk of her life has not yet happened. She'll dream about you frequently but won't have any idea why. And she'll al- ways sleep better."

"Why?"

"She's been kissed by an angel, silly. She'll imagine she's only remembering that special summer. And whenever she's genuinely happy, your image will drift into her thoughts. You'll always remain in her heart."

"What about everything else we did?"

"Such as?"

"The fifty thousand bucks. Nadine's cancer disappearing. How will things be explained?"

"The fireworks I saw in town were quite entertaining. Niemus suffered a nervous collapse and will be in the hospital for several weeks. When he recovers he'll have every single bank employee laboring over his accounts. The way he spends money, it'll take them forever to wade through the mess. He'll gather up all his canceled checks, have his accountants examine everything and make phone calls to everyone he's ever done business with. When his under-the-counter deals surface, he'll back off and reconsider what he's doing. To make things worse, his wife is back in town."

"That ought to steam up the situation a notch."

"There's also a boyfriend in the picture. A much younger man.

Niemus' wife has been just as unfaithful to Niemus as he's been to her. This young man has a substance abuse problem, which will add fuel to the fire. The picture will be hilarious. It's a shame we won't be here to watch it."

"What about Nadine's husband?"

"He's already having problems of his own. That clumsy attempt at check forgery, for instance. And since his big moneymaking scheme fell through and Nadine will soon file for divorce, he'll just disappear."

"She'll be much better off."

"She'll return to her doctor because she'll feel much better and wonder if something's wrong. The doctor will no longer see anything and assume the technician accidentally switched test results— something that happens all the time. He'll tell Nadine about the mistake and will reprimand the technician."

"What about her house? She'll be expecting them to take it from her."

"When she doesn't hear from her bank she'll most definitely get in touch. They'll send her the papers with the mortgage paid in full."

"I don't understand."

"Neither will Nadine. But when they examine her account, everything will balance."

"How can that be?"

Harriet just smiled.

"I think I get it."

"Mortals are ridiculously easy to work with. We're dealing with incompetence, attitudes, personalities, temperaments. The fact that they're so easily confused takes some of the challenge out of this."

"But won't all this mess with her mind?"

"She'll be all right. She's honest, not stupid. When she goes through her books and finds nothing but balances, it'll be enough for her. In time she'll wonder if it actually happened in the first place."

"What about the foreclosure notice?"

"Haven't you ever mislaid something important? And after several hours of looking for it, it turned up in the first place you looked?"

"Sure, but—"

"And other things you were looking for, just as important, you never found?"

"A few times…"

"Did you remember what *those* items were?"

"I'll be damned. I've been visited before, haven't I?"

"That's what we do. You should know that by now."

"Was it you?"

"That's another thing we do."

"What's that?"

"We never tell."

Heavy white masses twisted sluggishly before them. Rand became pensive again, thinking about

Nadine. "So somewhere down the line, she'll find someone else," he said.

"There'll be someone—perhaps when she returns to medical school. He'll probably be much like you were in your younger days, and she'll be quite taken by him. She's much too pretty and too special to remain unattached. But she'll never forget you, or that special summer when she became a woman. Like I said, you'll always remain in her heart."

He didn't reply. Something
(*"much like you were"*)
she'd just said...

"What did you mean by that?" he asked.

"By what?"

"What I was like in my younger days?"

"Tell me what you think I meant."

Something was very strange about all this. The way she could read him even though he tried so hard to keep things inside. Those innuendoes. That flare of temper when they were talking about—

"You never did tell me who you talked to up there."

"Maybe I didn't actually talk to *any*one," she said, flicking her hair away from her face.

"Then...how would you...how would you know so much about me?"

"I would've thought you'd have it figured out by now. After all, you *are* able to learn things so *quickly*. And by the way, you always *were* a great kisser."

311

My God. He could barely read her expression as the clouds moved around her smooth features. *Stupid male pride. Your younger days. Great kisser. Lost love...*

But all the beautiful, unfamiliar face told him was that it wasn't real.

"Dammit. You're wearing a covering yourself."

"We didn't think you could handle it if you knew who I was. It would've been difficult for me as well."

There weren't that many women in his life—not as many as there might have been. In high school there were only two, in college just a handful of casual dates. As a musician there were groupies, all of them forgettable. And after Nadine, there were only three or four, nearly all of them just as casual as—

"Try Tampa," she said, the blue sapphires glinting.

Tampa. He'd been there just a few times for software conventions. There were only two notable things that had happened there: making as well as losing a valuable contact with SLJ DigiSoft, Ltd., owned by Sam Jennings and run by Connie, his only daughter—

Connie. The beautiful redhead who'd captured his heart five years ago. The woman he'd fled from as soon as their relationship took a turn in the wrong direction. Wrong direction. In those days that meant getting serious, moving in, sharing an apartment—all the things he was running away from.

Connie was the only woman he'd ever considered spending the rest of his life with.

But he'd made tracks as soon as he discovered he was falling for her.

"Look at me, Rand."

"I ...don't think I can." He was careful to keep his attention on the clouds around them. When he focused on them he wasn't as frightened or as angry. He was angry at himself for not knowing who this beautiful creature was, frightened by who she might actually be.

"Please?"

The long white hair immediately darkened, turning a glistening red, the sapphire blues a bright chestnut color. It was Connie. Harriet was Connie all along.

"My God...I should've known."

She smiled. "You really should have."

"H-How is it that you're—"

"I died a year after you walked out on me," she said. "It was a heart ailment. I'd had it all my life."

"But you were in such great shape..." She was sensational in a string bikini. And she loved to play tennis and golf, swim..."In fact—"

"Save it. No longer relevant."

"It wasn't...because of me, was it?"

"Not directly. But your walking out didn't help."

"I'm *so* sorry. I had no idea—"

"I know the story now."

"Do you?"

She nodded. "I hated you for the longest time, figured you were just another coward afraid of commitment. But after what I've seen, I no longer blame you. You were clinging so hard to that illusion, your head wasn't where it should have been."

"My head hasn't been on straight for a very long time."

"Now it is."

"A little late, isn't it?"

"Remember what Nadine said?"

"She said a lot."

"We would've been so good together."

"I remember."

"Well...now you can say that to *me*."

The clouds grew lighter.

"Do you remember that time you got drunk, jumped in the hotel pool with all your clothes on, then took a taxi over to our place and showed up at the door drenched from head to toe, holding a bouquet of horrible-looking roses you'd snatched from someone's garden on the way over? You were in a panic and told my father you'd been looking for me in the pool but couldn't find me."

"Didn't go over too well."

"He thought it was hilarious."

"Could've fooled *me*..."

"He didn't want to make it too easy."

"By the way, how's he doing?"

"Getting on up there, but as well as can be expected. I look in on him from time to time—just to see if he's behaving himself, of course."

"I wonder what he'd think if he knew about us right now…

"He'd die laughing."

"You think so?"

"He always liked you, you know. But he thought you were only after my body."

"I was."

"I knew that."

"Then why did you put up with me?"

"What do you think *I* was after?"

"I'm glad you still have that same warped sense of humor."

"A girl needs one around you."

"What was wrong with the roses?"

"Not much. Just that they were dead."

"No wonder they wouldn't stand up on their own." A thought occurred to him. "So why'd you put them in water?"

"You were so pitiful that night, I didn't think you would've been able to handle it if I just dumped them in the trash."

"I would've probably had a heart attack."

She laughed. "You sure were funny. Daddy even took pictures. We had them displayed on the mantle for months afterward. Whenever we needed a laugh, all we had to do was look at them."

"You really know how to hurt a dead guy."

She was still laughing as the clouds swallowed them up.

OTHER WORKS BY DAVID BERARDELLI

THE WAGON DRIVER
DEMON CHASER
DEMON CHASER II
STEPPING OUT OF MY GRAVE
ESCAPE CLAUSE
FATAL INNOCENCE
THE FUNNY DETECTIVE
JUST A SIMPLE ERRAND
COLORS
WORKING FOR A MOB BOSS
AND DARKNESS FELL
AFTER DARKNESS FELL
DEMON CHASER III
IN ANOTHER REALM
BEYOND RECOGNITION
THE NIGHTMARE COLLECTOR
HIDDEN
DEMON CHASER IV
BEYOND GUILT
A RIPPLE IN TIME
THE PLANNING COMMITTEE
WINTER SCENE
DEMON'D!
AWAKENED

Titles available through:
Fiction4All